I0709138

HARROWED HEARTS

LEIGHANN HART

This is a work of fiction. Names, characters, places, and incidents either are the product of the author's imagination or are used fictitiously. Any resemblance to actual persons, living or dead, events, or locales is entirely coincidental.

Copyright © Crooked Hart Press, LLC 2024

All rights reserved. No part of this book may be reproduced in any form by an electronic or mechanical means, including information storage and retrieval systems, without permission in writing from the publisher, except by a reviewer who may quote brief passages in a review.

First paperback edition December 2024

Cover Design © Books and Moods

Copy Edits by Justin Williams

ISBN 978-1-7376130-8-4

PLAYLIST

Work Song - Hozier
Pity Party - Melanie Martinez
Shake Me Down - Cage the Elephant
All I Want - Kodaline
The Sound of Silence - Simon & Garfunkel
I Will Follow You Into the Dark - Death Cab for Cutie
Running to the Edge of the World - Marilyn Manson
An Honest Mistake - The Bravery
Wake Up - Coheed and Cambria
Closer - Nine Inch Nails
Fineshrine - Purity Ring
I Will Follow Him - Peggy March
Doubt - Twenty One Pilots
Heavy in Your Arms - Florence + The Machine
Roses and Sacrifice - The Avett Brothers
Dark Times - The Weeknd, Ed Sheeran
Are You Lonesome Tonight - Elvis Presley
10,000 Emerald Pools - BORNS
Mess Is Mine - Vance Joy
All These Things That I've Done - The Killers
Strangers - Lucius
Dark Side - Phoebe Ryan
All Who Remain - Beware of Darkness
Gone Forever - Three Days Grace
Big Fat Mouth - Arlie
Fix You - Valentin, Adeena, caravan
You're Mine - Phantogram
Always Forever - Cults
Run From Me - Timber Timbre

Why Don't You Try - Leonard Cohen
Sinking Man - Of Monsters and Men
Take a Slice - Glass Animals
Everybody Loves Somebody - Dean Martin
I Walk the Line - Johnny Cash
Mariners Apartment Complex - Lana Del Rey

"You are the knife I turn inside myself;
this is love.
This, my dear, is love."

— **Franz Kafka,** *Letters to Milena*

April

1

SAVE YOUR PENANCE

Dayton

No one clapped. No one cried. Least of all them.

Kenna was better suited for the role of cringing captive than blushing bride, studying the engagement ring as if it had been excavated from a jar of preserved organs. For Dayton, her reaction was secondary to her answer.

And, in spite of her hesitance, she had said yes.

He was on cloud nine. Brassy jazz wailed from the house band's instruments. It served as an overture to his personal triumph moments before. She sipped her wine, the diamonds glowing under the restaurant's dim lighting. Everything was perfect.

Until she had the gall to sully his contentment.

"Your timing is disturbing, although that's not much of a surprise."

Dayton tensed in his seat. "Is something the matter?"

He took in the sight of her red-rimmed eyes. He'd been so astounded by her cooperation with the night's events that he had temporarily forgotten she was an emotional wreck when she'd joined him at Sinclair's.

Zoning out on the wine bottle, she confided, "It involves the day I didn't want to talk about."

It seemed to him that she feared elaboration might condemn her further than the thousand dollar tourniquet he'd placed on her finger.

She was beautiful in her indecision. He said nothing. Watching, listening. Their meals were delivered with a nauseating degree of care and a symphony of silverware against porcelain filled the air between them before Kenna laid her knife down and tossed him a verbal hand grenade.

"Last night, I slept in my car."

"Why on Earth—"

"I was evicted."

In his mind, the room went still, every movement and every breath suspended. He could've rejoiced at her folly. Oh, he could've. Instead, fury crawled up his throat and tinged his whisper. "Why didn't you call me? Or do you not deem teetering on the edge of homelessness an emergency?"

She speared a stalk of asparagus, biting half of it and chewing deliberately, eyes on the tablecloth like a child dodging admonishment from a parent.

"What about your roommate? Where is she?"

"That's why I was evicted. Liza moved out a few months ago. Courtesy of you." Her eyes met his and, despite their puffy state, they had a sharpness that had him intimidated in the presence of a woman for the first time. "She said you were coming around when I wasn't home. So she left."

Seconds ticked by as he wrestled with how he wanted to play this. Their engagement bound them in a way that went beyond casual attachment, and served to protect them both. Honesty, he realized, was more precious now than ever.

"I admit I was there on more than one occasion."

A small smile graced her lips. "This isn't confessional, Dayton. Save your penance." That smile faded as she propped her elbows on the table, arms folded. "I don't care that you were in my apartment. I don't care *why* you were there. But you have to understand that as a result of you showing up unannounced and making Liza feel unsafe, I now need a place to stay." She held up her hand like a seasoned jewelry model. "And this ring says you're it."

It has been said that good things come in threes.

Kenna was his fiancée. She was, apparently, moving in with him. He prayed the third thing involved Shane Sanders.

2

BURN IT

Kenna

*C*hoices shape one's life.

Kenna considered all of the wrong ones she'd made that had culminated in the diamond on her finger and living with the monster of a man she loved.

They fit the bill of warden and prisoner better than a newly engaged couple. Couple. She loved Dayton and, still, the word made her cringe. No, they were simply two people bound by the nefarious whims of consequence and circumstance.

She considered this while staring at her flashy engagement ring as he brought another box of her belongings into his house. Kenna supposed, with a great deal of repugnance, that it was now *their* house.

"That's everything," he said with an air of gentleness.

Amazingly, he wasn't smug in the face of her eviction. The soft edge in his gaze communicated that he understood she'd need time to settle in and adjust to the magnitude of these changes. It wasn't common for people to go from hardly dating to being engaged to living under the same roof within a 48-hour window.

She perched on the arm of the sofa, leaning forward, arms folded across her knees. Dayton tossed his keys onto the coffee table and picked up a pile of mail, sorting through it. She wondered how he was able to do that—carry on with his life and function in any capacity in spite of all of the pain and suffering he'd inflicted.

He spoke without looking away from the envelopes.

"I cleared some space in the dresser as well as the closet. I'd be happy to move around some of my things if you need more room."

Dayton employed the same clean-cut manner of speaking he defaulted to with patients and, for some reason, she was hurt by it. Had she any other option, she wouldn't have moved into 673 Fairbrook, yet the idea that its owner may not have wanted her around sent her stomach into knots.

She felt out of sorts in the house knowing she was there to stay, as if she'd won a competition with no willing participants and she was reluctantly claiming her prize.

His mouth pulled into a frown as he consulted the time. He went into the bedroom, emerging minutes later dressed in his usual wares: slacks and a button-down. He swiped his Owens-Adair ID badge off the side table and clipped it to his shirt pocket. Though he'd rescheduled the day's appointments at the practice to help her move in, there was no getting around his shift at the emergency room.

It was part of his weekly routine. His ritual.

Dayton sighed and regarded her like an enigma; something to be solved, rather than a living creature.

"I have to go." He pressed a kiss to her cheek and pulled back. "Sorry we can't spend the evening together."

Kenna had to forcibly stop herself from laughing. He was almost treating her like a fiancée instead of a hostage.

The front door clicked shut and she released a dramatic sigh.

Fingers sinking into her hair, she stared at the brown leather cushion beneath her feet. It was the second occasion on which she'd been left alone in his house and she reeled at the dramatic shift with so little passage of time.

She was a resident, no longer a guest.

In a matter of weeks, she would sign a paper and become Kenna O'Callaghan-Merino. She was relieved exam week was around the corner; it meant she could delay updating her address with the university until fall term. The despair that would inevitably accompany that small change was far off but she already dreaded the interaction with the registrar personnel. Would they remember that Dayton lived on the same street? Worse yet, would they cross-reference his old file for curiosity's sake and discover that it was not only the same street, but the same address?

Kenna pushed herself off the sofa's arm, realizing it wouldn't do her any good to worry over what was out of her control. Closing her eyes, she took a deep, grounding breath and when she opened them, they panned around at her new home—*their* home. Butterflies brushed the undersides of her ribs as the reality sank in.

Dayton was gone for the next nine hours and, as much as she wanted to search the place top to bottom, she thought the idea was unwise. If she came across something repulsive, she couldn't run away.

For she had nowhere to go.

Instead, Kenna carried the bags and boxes containing her clothes to the bedroom. Johnny Cash's soothing, low register played from her phone as she took her time hanging things up. Others, she folded and carefully tucked away in the dresser. As she closed one of the drawers, she noticed a large candle sitting atop the dresser, with a lighter off to the side. The jar was black, free of a logo or any kind of text. No sooner than she lifted it and read the bottom label did she regret picking it up. Dayton's print-cursive scrawl stared back at her.

Welcome home, kid. Burn it.

A lump formed in her throat as she quickly replaced it. Whether it was sincere or his idea of a practical joke, it left her unsettled. Once the lump had alleviated itself, she realized what an odd request it was, asking her to burn a candle as if it weren't self-explanatory. Her muscles stiffened as she caught sight of the sharp white corners peeking out beneath the edge of the jar.

She retrieved the paper only to discover it wasn't a paper at all but a Polaroid, the one with the damning inscription that had sent her to the bottom of this rabbit hole. Coming face to face with that photograph felt like standing on the grass and peering down into that deep, dark abyss. A full-circle moment—though she was no closer to the truth that had hurled her to the bottom.

Holding the picture of herself in a trembling hand, she was greeted with unpleasant flashbacks of rifling through his little box of horrors. It fluttered to the floor and Kenna knelt to pick it up. She was done succumbing to that fear.

It wasn't that they were playing by new rules. Rather, the game had changed entirely.

For a beat, she regarded the lighter and imagined the ephemeral joy it might bring to send that photo up in smoke.

But then she studied her pajamas nestled beside his running clothes in an open drawer, her jeans hanging next to his slacks in the closet, and an unexpected air of calm settled over her. This was really happening.

She was living with Dr. Merino.

She was his *fiancée.*

Despite all of the hurt that Polaroid and all of its friends had brought her, revenge had never truly been on Kenna's agenda. The universe had carved out her fate one cold January morning in Markham Hall. She was reborn in that office. Sired within seconds to a man whom she'd never met.

The diamonds gleamed in the fading daylight streaming

through the window. She felt the ghost of his kiss on her wrist after he'd slid the ring onto her finger.

You're mine now, lamb. It was a truth that burning a photograph wouldn't change.

Kenna wandered into the kitchen, wondering begrudgingly if she would find Rohypnol among the stash of cooking ingredients. She examined the space whose details she had failed to take serious note of during previous visits. Cobalt walls and a white subway tile backsplash. Butcher-block counters. Dayton was neat but not to a fault. His mug of tea from that morning remained on the dinner table. The drying rack was full but other dishes lingered in the sink.

She raided the kitchen in search of alcohol, finding none. Its absence shouldn't have come as a surprise. Medically speaking, he wasn't allowed to drink.

The wine he'd used as a cover to drug her must have been purchased specially for the occasion. Kenna grew sick thinking of all the women he had entertained in that kitchen. Their faces were forever branded in her memory.

Bracing her hands on the counter, she focused on her breathing. Deep breaths flooded her lungs, in and out, until she decided she was sufficiently calm. Getting caught up in all that had happened in the house every time she entered a room was not an option.

If she expected to carry on with her life somewhat peacefully under this roof, she'd have to come to terms with its phantoms.

A dull pain spread in her chest. A loneliness that knew no depth. More than anything, she wanted to video call her sisters, to show them the house, the ring. To pretend for a short while that she was happy without complication. Not that her sisters knew what a video call was.

She dismissed the idea.

The evening was growing late and dinner was in order. Her hand curled around the chrome handle on the fridge, pulling it open with a smack, and she regarded the well-stocked shelves in awe. While she'd lived with Alex—and later Liza—the inside of their refrigerator had always been a pitiful sight.

She made a smoked gouda grilled cheese and sat alone at the dining table, eating in silence. The sound of her chewing cut through the silence in a way that made her feel as if she were locked away in a padded cell, with nothing but the machination of a slowly disintegrating mind.

After brewing a cup of tea, Kenna settled in the living room, fanning her textbooks and notes out on the coffee table. Her attempt to study for finals did not last long. The aroma of chocolate mint wafted up from the mug, clinging to the air. She remembered when Dayton had feigned innocence and made her the same tea in hopes she'd feel better all the while knowing she was coming down off a mild dose of GHB.

The ring grew heavier on her finger at the memory.

Grabbing her tea off the side table, she noticed, for the first time, the apple candle he had burned that night resting beside the lamp. All at once, she was haunted by the sweetness of the apple-scented wax mixing with the spices of his cooking, and as she sat there, she couldn't recall a single memory in the house that wasn't riddled with anxiety.

Living there meant unease.

As much as she loved Dayton, she understood chances were slim that she'd ever feel truly comfortable around him. A part of her was disheartened by this. Wasn't comfort the very thing people sought out when searching for a partner?

Though, Kenna hadn't gone looking for a relationship.

It had just happened.

Perhaps tying herself to Dayton had been God's will. If that were the case, she would have given anything to be clued in on His reasoning.

Rising from the sofa, she made no motion to clean up her books, retreating to the rear of the house.

She ran a hot bath. The mirror fogged up as she peeled off her clothes and let them fall to the tile. The sting of the hot water enveloping her skin was the first semblance of relaxation she'd felt since stepping over the threshold.

Her lids fluttered shut and, after a round of deep breathing to further calm herself, she fell into an accidental but blissful sleep that quieted her overactive mind. Everything was black. Tranquil.

The sensation of falling overtook her and Kenna jolted awake, all flailing limbs and gasping breaths. She had no idea how much time had passed since she'd drifted off but the water had lost its heat and her cheek was branded pink from its extended contact with the side of the tub.

Through her exhaustion, she managed to climb out of the bath, towel off, and locate some pajamas. She was grateful for having put her clothes away, however unwilling she had been to do so.

A plume of wonderful scents broke free from the sheets as she collapsed on the bed. Lavender, vanilla, and the lingering petrichor from Dayton's sessions in the garden.

That familiarity embraced her like an old friend and carried her off to sleep.

The next time she opened her eyes, darkness still ruled over the room. As her vision adjusted, Kenna regarded the ceiling, not a sound save for her shallow breath.

Until she listened more closely.

There was a distant noise, coming from the main area of the house. The repetitive clicking of laptop keys. Scrubbing a hand across her face, she leaned over and checked the time on her phone, grimacing at its brightness.

4:27 a.m. Dayton had been home for hours.

Why hadn't he come to bed?

She wrapped up in the covers once more. Whatever he was doing was none of her concern; never mind their engagement.

She'd learned on many occasions that meddling in his private life only resulted in further complication.

Kenna was finished with complications.

She would be civil, and above all behaved, until the Greene murder trial happened—whether it was Shane Sanders or Dayton who took the stand—and then, regardless of the outcome, she'd file for divorce and do the sensible thing. Move on with her life.

True, she loved him. So much, it hurt. So much, she was sure she had never known love before him.

But staying with someone who used the looming prospect of a murder trial as leverage for a proposal acceptance wasn't her idea of happily ever after.

No matter how much she willed sleep to come, her eyes remained wide open. The typing seemed to pick up speed as she stared at the wall and, reluctantly, she shed her blanket cocoon. The hardwood was cool on her bare feet as she tiptoed into the living room.

No overhead light or lamp was on; there was only the glow of the screen, shining like an orb in the dark.

For a moment, she stood still, admiring the concentration on Dayton's weary face. His medical bracelet hit the desk softly with every keystroke and created a gentle jangling.

She remembered he had been on his laptop when she'd biked to his house in the middle of the night. Perhaps it was part of his routine. After all, she could count on one hand the number of times she'd stayed over. She knew very little about his habits at home.

"You're nocturnal. That explains a lot," she said.

Kenna thought he'd jump, alarmed by her presence, but instead he slowly turned to look at her, like he'd known she was standing there all along.

His middle finger pushed a key and the open tab disappeared, black eyes cutting to her. "Was that a joke?"

"I think so, yes."

"There are a few things I need to finish. I'll be in soon, unless you'd rather I sleep out here."

She swallowed, feeling as though she had betrayed herself, because despite how messed up their situation was, she didn't want him sleeping anywhere if it wasn't next to her.

Of course, she didn't tell him that.

"It's your house. You should be able to sleep in your own bed."

As she padded back toward the bedroom, she pretended not to hear the cursed words he whispered to no one in particular.

"*Our* house."

ONE OF THE REASONS

Dayton

Kenna's Polaroid was propped against the lamp on his nightstand. The photo stared back at him.

Her vibrant tresses sprawled on the black sheets. Skin so light it bordered on transparent. The lacy undergarments that kept her modesty at a bare minimum.

Dayton snatched the photo, studying it more closely as he lay in bed, adjusting to the daylight. He remembered making minor adjustments to her form that night. He'd fanned out her red hair, just so. Come time to take the picture, he had gazed upon her face, serene in its slumber, and considered carefully removing the lingerie, but decided against it.

Disrobing a saint was a cardinal sin.

Pinning the photo between his palm and chest, he wondered why Kenna hadn't burned it. She had returned it to him. Was it a message? Some kind of sign?

He intended to ask her but a quick glance revealed an empty mattress. The floor creaked lightly beneath his weight as he tugged a shirt over his head and left the bedroom in search of the woman with whom—through a series of fortunate events—he now cohabitated.

She sat crisscross on the couch, computer in her lap, buried in homework as usual. Dayton had no intention of starting an argument on their first full day living together, but he desperately wanted an explanation for what she'd left on his nightstand.

He extended the picture toward her. "What's this?"

She hardly looked up from the screen.

"Burning a photo won't undo the last year." Raising her eyebrows, she scrolled along her page. "And let me stop you before you say something trite like, 'Oh, but Kenna, burning it could be cathartic.' We both know these feelings will never go away."

His heart pumped its slow but steady, artificial rhythm and he waited out the silence, for he sensed she had something more to say.

"I can't believe you tried to give it to me in the first place. Isn't it part of your … process?"

The steady pumping ceased. Had she been up all night raiding the files on his laptop? He knew this moment was inevitable, but it was much too soon for her to loathe him in a way that was beyond all hope of redemption. Charlotte finding Humbert's diary. Didn't Kenna realize she was Dolores?

His light, his fire.

Resolving to be polite, he pocketed the Polaroid and squared his shoulders. "It's too early for this kind of discussion. Have you eaten?"

"How nice. He feeds his prisoners."

There went his civility.

"Damn it, Kenna. Don't act as if I'm holding you hostage here. I may have given you a reason to accept my proposal but, at the end of the day, you're the one who accepted it. And do you know what? I've racked my brain, going through every possibility, and each time I came to the incredibly obvious conclusion that you allowing me to slide that ring on your finger could only mean one thing. You love me. You're afraid to say it, so you don't. But I see it. In your eyes, more than anything in your eyes." His voice fractured, adopting a higher pitch which he chased away by clearing his throat. "How is it that you can love me and simultaneously have this contempt for me?"

While Kenna had been focused on her laptop before, the device was entirely forgotten during his monologue. It had fallen to the area rug and she made no bid to retrieve it. Her attention ping-ponged from Dayton to the coffee table in what felt like a never-ending loop.

It drove him wild, the muteness and fleeting glances.

A foul irritation simmered below his skin, begging to be personified as shouting or shaking her senseless. He expected her to raise her voice but when she spoke, she sounded tired and altogether uninterested.

"Please. What you're doing now is no different from your work. You're proposing a possible explanation based on observable behavior." She pushed herself off the couch, tipping her head in passing on the way to the kitchen. "Try as you may, you'll never be able to observe what's going through my head."

A laugh died in his throat, coming out as a shallow exhalation. "I know. It's one of the reasons I love you."

Whatever task she was preparing to delve into was rendered irrelevant as she froze upon hearing his words. Though her back was to him, he took great delight in picturing her reaction. Bewitching eyes staring helplessly at the backsplash. Mouth in that taut, neutral line that meant she was one inch of provocation away from unleashing the rage which she kept so expertly stoppered.

Squatting, Kenna rummaged through the lower cabinets, moving on to the next and then the next in quick succession. "Do you have a coffee maker?"

"No. Whenever I make decaf, I use instant. Didn't you bring one from your place?"

"We had an espresso machine. It was Liza's so, naturally, she took it when you scared her off."

Her position faltered and she resorted to crawling around on her hands and knees, still on the hunt even though he'd told her there was nothing to find. Meddlesome, as always. Dayton understood his response window was ticking by but he became engrossed in the gorgeous woman on his kitchen floor.

She wore brown terrycloth shorts that hugged her backside. As a byproduct of his gratuitous gazing, he was forced to readjust himself in his loungewear.

He decided to put them out of their collective misery.

Swiping a grocery bag off the top of the fridge, he said, "I'm well aware of your affinity for caffeine, which is why I picked this up on the way home last night."

Kenna peered inside, delicately scooping up the medium roast as if it were a precious gemstone. Any mark of anxiety fled her face and she regarded him with an openness that left him in want of her marvelous mouth.

Clutching the instant coffee to her chest, she said, "Thank you. I really needed this, with exams looming this week and, well, everything else."

All of the things he wished to say welled on his tongue. None were vocalized. They had no place amid their innocuous morning commentary, no matter his need to express them.

He didn't offer a 'you're welcome' or embrace her or steal a kiss. Rather, Dayton steeled his features and took a step toward the living room. He lingered there for a beat, examining her as if to confirm her presence in this place where he'd lived alone for so many years.

Sometimes he feared Kenna was an apparition, and for this reason—however illogical—he feared getting too close to her. She would be lost to his rapture.

"I'm going to head out for a run. Can you handle the kettle?"

"I think I can manage."

Tiny shards of glass nestled against his heart as her eyes swept away from him. It was a grating sensation, a painful itch that refused to abate even as he ducked into the bedroom and hastily changed.

Pausing on the mat by the front door, he said, "Carmen's coming into town at the end of the week. To help plan the wedding."

Kenna ceased all movement.

"We've been engaged for a few days. How could she have possibly taken time off work on such short notice?"

"Because, darling," he called, halfway out the door, producing a smile that he hoped was equally charming and disarming, "I knew you'd say yes."

May

$$4$$

NOTHING MORE

Kenna

Kenna was used to the comments and snide remarks. The stares, however, were new, ushered in no doubt by the rock on her hand that she'd stared at for five minutes while getting ready, and had ultimately come to the conclusion that she couldn't remove it. Dayton had put it there, and there it would remain. Until the divorce he'd agreed to was filed, of course. Until then, she was his.

Body, mind, and soul.

Besides, removing a ring for a few hours wouldn't improve the reputation she'd garnered on campus.

Though, perhaps her classmates would be less scandalized knowing the dark doctor intended to make an honest woman out of her.

Kenna had no such luck. No matter how engaging she believed her behavior pathology presentation to be, everyone's attention seemed to collectively home in on her left hand, completely disregarding her carefully curated slideshow and the talking points she'd tirelessly rehearsed. Her blood boiled at having her project upstaged by a piece of jewelry, which may as well have been wailing and flashing like an emergency vehicle's siren. She only hoped her professor hadn't been as distracted by it.

As she exited the classroom, she bumped into a forlorn Will Morris. His mood seemed to extend to his hair as well, coif of curls looking deflated. The right side of his jaw worked in sluggish movements, likely chewing a piece of gum. While she was in no mood for chitchat, she also wasn't in the habit of turning people away, which is why she made no protest when Will spoke.

"Pretty sure I bombed Dr. Kim's exam."

Kenna offered a polite smile in greeting, but kept moving in the direction of her next class. "She's tough, but fair, from what I remember."

He looked over his shoulder. "You're coming from Allen, huh? How'd that go?"

"Presentations. We had a cumulative project in place of an exam, which, honestly, I prefer over a test any day."

"I get that. Then you feel like you at least have some control over how it turns out, and your fate isn't sealed by face-melting hours of studying or what you overlook come time for the exam."

Kenna actually laughed. The rare, whole body, burning sides kind of laughter. Coincidentally, she hadn't laughed like that since the last time she'd seen Will, but he had not been the one to elicit it. It had been Dayton, in his parked car, when one minute she considered running away and the next she reveled in his nearness and his effortless charm. That juxtaposition summarized their entire relationship quite nicely.

Will's attention dipped below her face and she was momentarily offended until she realized what had him rapt; the thing she had already grown tired of people noticing.

"Oh wow," he said. She failed to discern the nature of his expression, and she grew uncomfortable the longer the silence stretched on between them in the middle of the crowded hallway. "When did this happen?"

"Last week."

"Congratulations, Kenna. I'm happy for you."

"Do you really mean that?"

Something twinkled in his blue eyes. "You love him, don't you?"

Her chest went tight. She knew the answer. It wasn't something she had to think about. But would she admit it to Will Morris when she'd never spoken the words to her own fiancé?

"I do."

"Then yes, I mean it. Wholeheartedly." He leaned in, whispering conspiratorially with his cinnamon gum breath, "But I still think he's a huge asshole."

"I'd be worried if you didn't."

Amusement came over Will's face. Laughing, he rubbed the back of his neck. "Oh man, wait 'til Liam hears the news. He will absolutely freak."

"Ms. O'Callaghan," came a familiar voice, "just the young lady I wanted to see."

Kenna turned and there stood Dean Raza, same as ever with his bold brows and pitiful black toupee. He ignored Will entirely.

"Tell me, when is your next exam?"

"10:15, sir."

The dean gave a single nod and began walking away, gesturing with a raised hand for her to follow. "I'd like to speak with you in my office."

Memories of the meeting with Dayton ushered forth as she was faced with the ghastly drapes and intricate Persian rug. That had been the point of no return. Alice's dark descent into Wonderland.

A spiteful part of her wished she'd turned elsewhere for a mentor, but her heart insisted things ended up exactly as they were supposed to, that they were meant to find each other.

That all of this was preordained.

And while Kenna had no way of knowing if that was true, romanticizing her current reality was the only thing that gave her the strength to get out of bed every morning.

Without that rose-colored lens, she was a girl who was half as clever as she thought. A girl who harbored feelings for an insidious beast. A girl who betrayed her own family.

Throat stinging, she forced herself to look Dean Raza in the eye. She wouldn't spare Dayton, nor anything else, another thought.

All that mattered was the man behind the desk and uncovering the reason why he'd sequestered her in his office.

He caught a glimpse of her ring, mumbling an exasperation in Arabic before addressing her in their common language. "There's no easy way to break into this, although, firstly I should tell you this has nothing to do with your academic performance. You've made the dean's list every semester. You're one of our top students, which is why this situation distresses me a great deal."

As soon as he said 'situation,' she understood perfectly well why she was there. Everything always led back to Dayton.

It was Professor Henrick telling her all over again that she'd have to redo her practicum if she had any desire to graduate, her romantic choices once again landing her in hot water. Irritation heated her neck, for she knew if it were a male student in this scenario, a meeting of this variety would not have taken place.

"Make no mistake. I want you to succeed, but Ponderosa has nothing more to offer. Your presence at the university has become a problem. I held out hope that eventually the storm would pass, so to speak, but the incident between Dr. Merino and yourself has had a tremendous effect on the student body. An effect, I'm afraid, that has not waned. A scandal of this magnitude is not only a great disturbance for the faculty and students, but it bleeds beyond our grounds. It can damage the school's reputation."

However politely the dean put it, there was no mistaking his words. She was being kicked out.

An iciness sheathed her forearms, spreading to her shoulders and coiling around her heart. The weight of it had her on the brink of hyperventilation. All of the recent events compounded and Dean Raza's decision broke her.

She'd been ousted from her apartment as well as her school, and though she had found another place to live, finding another university would be a trickier matter.

"I cannot ask you to leave in any official capacity. I'm hoping that this conversation is impetus enough. You are nothing short of brilliant, Ms. O'Callaghan. I have connections at plenty of universities across the Pacific Northwest and I'd have no objection to writing a letter of recommendation."

"Yes, sir. I understand." The words were spoken so softly, she wasn't entirely sure they'd come out of her mouth.

"Consider everything I've said today and provide me with a list of schools at your earliest convenience. The sooner we get the ball rolling, the better chance you'll have of your graduate program continuing without interruption."

Kenna said nothing further, rising gracefully from the leather chair. Dean Raza had stripped her of everything and she exited his office parading what she was beneath all that hair and skin.

A hollow frame with a faulty conscience.

5

WHITE SATIN

Kenna

*D*ays had passed and Dean Raza's proposition had only grown heavier. It was a miracle Kenna managed to put it out of her mind long enough to get through exams. She wondered how long it might take her to drum up the list of schools he'd requested. Foregoing the list altogether was appealing, leaving the university behind without a single care. She'd forge her own path and, besides, they wanted her gone. What gave them any right to know where she started anew?

At the red light, Kenna centered her breathing.

She was being ungrateful. Raza could have expelled her for all she knew, but he kept the whole affair quiet and even offered to help her get into a different university.

The light changed and she went straight rather than turning left for the practice. Dayton had hired a temp for exam week. Though she didn't express it outwardly, she was relieved when he told her.

She did a double take pulling into the driveway when she spotted Carmen perched on the porch steps. Before Kenna had a chance to cut the engine, she was knocking on the driver's side window. She cracked the door since that was infinitely easier than wrestling with the manual crank.

Carmen's dark hair was woven into a fishtail braid, which slid over one of her shoulders as she leaned down to address Kenna. "I kept calling and calling this place and I finally got you an appointment but we have to leave like yesterday."

Brain thoroughly fried after the last few weeks of studying, she tried to make sense of what Carmen was saying. "An appointment? What for?"

"Are you deaf? Let's go. I'll explain on the way."

"It's best if you drive, then. If we're in a hurry."

Climbing over the console, she plopped into the passenger seat and yanked the seatbelt across her chest. Carmen, on the other hand, drove halfway down Fairbrook before giving any thought to putting hers on. Kenna didn't question her urgency, at first, mentally drained from the day and overwhelmed at being chauffeured to an unknown destination. She knew Carmen was there to expedite the wedding planning and assumed wherever they were rushing off to was somehow related.

"I was surprised to see you when I got home. Dayton didn't tell me which day you were getting here, just that you were coming at the end of the week."

Her brows flexed faintly. "That's my brother for you."

"What kind of appointment is this?"

"For your dress. We better hope they have something your size on the rack. The wedding's, what, a month away? There's no way they can special order a gown within that kind of time frame."

One month.

Kenna glanced out the window and instantly regretted it as she watched the scenery blur past at Carmen's breakneck speed. A nasty bout of motion sickness threatened to do her in. She figured there would be a quick turnaround for their marriage due to the ongoing investigation, that harbinger of ill-fated matrimonial unions, but a month seemed terribly sudden.

"You know a lot about weddings."

"Unwanted knowledge, believe me. My girlfriend is a complete TLC junkie. I swear she's seen every episode of *Say Yes to the Dress* three times."

No amount of careful consideration made the words sound any better in her head. She tried anyway. "I didn't realize you were—"

Carmen's usual cheerful expression sobered. "Now it's not so hard to see why Dayton's the favorite twin, huh? Aside from the obvious fact that he's a doctor."

"So your parents know?"

"We haven't talked about it in so many words but I'm sure they've figured it out by now."

"I think it's brave you still interact with them, knowing that they might not accept who you are. I ran away when my family wouldn't accept me, and now I worry that if I decide to go back one day, they won't open that door I walked out of."

A heavy silence hung in the air. The sky progressively darkened as they neared Portland, brimming with the ever-present threat of afternoon rain. Kenna studied the charcoal clouds with feigned interest. Meanwhile, she worried whether she'd overstepped some sort of invisible boundary until Carmen finally spoke.

"Family is family, no matter what." Her inky eyes flicked to Kenna. "You'll always have a place with the Merinos."

Dayton

Dayton considered it a miracle that his cell phone had not gone off. He thought Kenna would've been furious to be whisked away by his sister on a dress-shopping mission, but hours ticked by and he heard nothing from either of them.

Later in the evening, once he was rid of patients, he met

Nathan at the men's formal-wear shop downtown. The stylist caught him off guard with a question about wedding colors, in hopes of coordinating ties and pocket squares, and he was met with the realization that he hadn't the slightest idea what kind of colors Kenna liked.

"Black will work for everything."

Her heavily made-up face all but crumpled in despair as she went off in search of the drab accessories. Betty, a name that belied her age, put up less resistance when he requested black tuxedos and dress shirts.

Nathan emerged from the dressing room, examining the fit in the oversized mirror. "Seems like we were just doing this for my wedding."

"For me, it feels like another lifetime." Dayton took a few paces toward him. Scanning his friend head to toe, he assessed every seam and stitch. "The jacket's a little loose. You'll need to get it altered."

Nathan turned to face him. "Can I ask you one thing?"

He opened his mouth to deliver a biting remark but Betty appeared, pinstriped pocket squares in hand, and she took the brunt of his irritation.

"What part of solid aren't you grasping, Beatrice?"

She retreated with a childish humph.

"Don't get me wrong—I'm over the moon for you. It's a miracle you found a girl who can tolerate you. But you guys have been engaged for how long? A *week*? And here we are putting rush orders on tuxedos."

"The point, Nate."

"Why are you rushing this? You guys have your whole lives ahead of you. She'll be done with school in another year. Have you entertained the idea of waiting until then?"

Sure, he'd entertained the idea. Before Lacey Greene had come pounding on the windows of his practice. He'd imagined genuine love and the possibility that, one day, Kenna would marry him of her own volition. But their fate had panned out differently. He was certain that, though she may have loved him, she wanted none of this and would run from him the first chance she got. She cared enough to protect him but not enough to remain at his side once the threat of incarceration dissipated.

For now, Dayton counted his blessings every morning he woke up next to her, whether she loved or despised him.

"Kenna and I love each other in a way I think most people aren't capable of understanding, and I won't wait longer than necessary to claim her before the eyes of God. I want the world to know that she's mine."

Scrunching his forehead, Nathan continued his lecture. "Women aren't property. She may love your crazy ass but she's only yours as long as she wants to be. Remember that. And treat her right. That girl's been through hell this last year because of you."

"No, Nathaniel." Straightening his suit jacket, he met Nathan's eyes in the mirror. "We've put each other through hell."

Kenna

Kenna braced her palms against the wall as the consultant tugged on the gown's laces, gracing her with more cleavage than she thought possible while also squeezing every last ounce of breath from her lungs. She was surprised speech had not abandoned her in her oxygen-deprived state.

"Is it supposed to be this tight?"

"First time in anything corseted? I promise you, honey, first or fortieth, it doesn't get any more comfortable. It'll do wonders for your figure, though. I promise you that."

Cheryl pulled on the laces a final time and Kenna winced before steeling her features as the ends were swiftly tied into a bow and she was let out into the fitting room's guest lounge.

Inhaling as much as the boning would allow, Kenna gathered

the skirt and stepped onto a platform that faced a wall of mirrors. She released the material bunched in her hands, staring at the girl in those many panels.

With a bare face and tousled hair, she looked too young, too inexperienced to don such an elegant dress.

Truthfully, she was.

Her substance was of no importance. The wedding would happen regardless. And though she loved Dayton something fierce —loath as she was to admit it and vile as that love was—she wished they didn't have to rush into marriage.

Carmen studied her for a long moment, never breaking eye contact as she snagged an energy drink out of her bag and cracked it open with an audible *pop*, much to the chagrin of Cheryl, who had offered them complimentary champagne upon their arrival. Carmen leaned back on the sofa and took a gratuitous swig before releasing a disappointed sigh.

"Honestly? This one's fucking gorgeous with a capital 'g,' but I think my parents would have heart attacks on the spot if you married their son in *this*."

"I'm glad you found some kind of fault with it."

Her face fell. "You really don't like it? I mean, you look amazing."

Giving herself a once-over in the mirror, Kenna decided that she liked the dress based on aesthetic alone. It was ballgown style, with a voluminous skirt composed of tulle and a silk lining. The bodice was sheer, floral lace that was revealing in a tasteful way.

"No, you're right. It's beautiful, but I wouldn't be able to draw enough breath to say my vows so, sadly, it's a resounding no."

Cheryl ushered her into the dressing room once again and unlaced the corset as efficiently as she had tied it.

Carmen raised her voice in order to be heard through the door. "He's already written his, you know. Don't tell him I told you that. God forbid anyone believes he's romantic under all his scowling."

This bit of information gave Kenna pause. Were the sake of

their union purely for legal strategy, writing vows ahead of time seemed at odds with the agenda. Unless, of course, she considered the very likely possibility that she'd bewitched the heart of a killer. The thought made her shiver and yet she did not run from the shop. She did not tear the engagement ring off her finger. Calmly, she indicated to Cheryl which dress she wanted to try on next.

Stepping into a mermaid gown, Kenna called out, "Oh, don't worry. I won't say a thing."

Before Cheryl had touched the zipper, Kenna knew the style didn't suit her. It accentuated her natural litheness in a manner that was decidedly unflattering. Once it had been secured, she opened the door and walked out to get Carmen's take.

A tense expression came over her, an equal blend of displeasure and confusion. "Jesus, I didn't know you were so—"

She hesitated the same way Kenna had in the car. Though, what Carmen had cut herself off from saying was perhaps far less offensive.

"Bony?"

"Well, yeah," Carmen said softly.

She had gone to the doctor months prior. While she'd lost a few pounds, he had assured her she was in no danger of being under-weight. Her lean frame paired with hip bones and shoulder blades that protruded slightly more than was normal seldom made her feel unattractive, but standing there looking at her reflection was one such occasion.

"I'm sure I'll put on some weight. After the wedding."

They were empty words of assurance. Domestic bliss wasn't in the cards. Sleepless nights, paranoia, and general unrest were more aligned with her expectations.

"I don't want to put any pressure on you, hun, but we've got another bride comin' in at 5. You can always schedule another appointment if you don't find anything you like today."

Carmen piped up in a way Kenna imagined a mother would in

such a situation. "We have to go home with a dress. Their wedding is June 12th."

"Good heavens." One of Cheryl's hands flew to her blonde, gray-streaked curls. "That's short notice. Practically last minute. You're just now looking for a gown?"

"We're very recently engaged."

"So, what's the big hurry?"

Kenna glanced at Carmen and wished she hadn't, for she manifested a look that was strikingly similar to the one she'd donned during Thanksgiving weekend, when their father had touched Dayton's face and he'd so easily brushed off his scars.

Was it possible she knew about Lacey?

"It's complicated," Kenna said as Cheryl escorted her into the dressing room for the umpteenth time.

She chuckled, removing the gown with little ease compared to its corseted predecessor. "You'd be mighty surprised at the stories I've heard over the years. Sometimes, being a bridal consultant feels like being a couples counselor."

"He and I weren't supposed to happen. It wasn't *allowed* to happen. We both paid the price." More to herself, Kenna muttered, "I'm still paying it, really."

"There's nothin' more romantic than forbidden love. Whatever reason you two have for tying the knot so quick, I'm sure it's a good one." Cheryl flung through the slim selection of remaining gowns on the rollaway rack, landing on one and eliciting a small but excited gasp. "I think you should try this one."

Kenna felt no spark of intrigue upon seeing the limp garment on the hanger. When she put it on, it was another story. Even in her bare feet, she'd never felt so elegant.

Carmen suffered an instance of verbal diarrhea that had Cheryl looking down her nose at the younger woman.

"Holy mother of fuck." She immediately signed the cross, mumbling something about forgiveness under her breath and then she was on her feet, lingering near where Kenna stood on the plat-form. "We'll take it."

The dress was simple in design yet luxurious, constructed entirely of charmeuse. Two fingers' width of silk banded over each shoulder. A well-disguised zipper ran along her left side and the skirt's material pooled at her feet without doing so in excess.

A faint smile brightened her face for a fraction of a second, the only happiness she allowed herself on this day, and then she turned to Carmen and Cheryl.

"It's the one."

On the way to Portland, their conversation had been free-flowing but an air of unease suffused the drive back to Branch Spring.

Kenna was saddened their outing had come to an end. Secretly, she relished the time with Carmen, the person who knew Dayton better than anyone—which was why she was also disappointed that she'd squeezed no useful information out of his twin, other than the troubling look in the dressing room.

Her pulse sped up, heart slamming against the walls of her chest. There was no time to regret her unspoken words before they fled her lips.

"If there's something you think I should know, I hope you'd tell me before I walk down the aisle."

"Dayton always tells me how much he loves your curiosity. I was starting to wonder if I'd ever see that side of you." Though Carmen's features didn't betray any emotion, her forearms tensed and her posture straightened. "Look, I'm not going to sit here and tell you he's a saint—because we both know that's far from the truth —but he's my brother and I'm not going to put him down, either. He has a past. You must know something about that by now."

Kenna sensed Carmen hadn't said all she wished to say, and so she remained quiet and patient in the hope that greater under-standing would follow.

"I'm glad he's getting a second shot at this. Hell, after Audrey, I didn't think he'd ever mess with an engagement again." A chill coiled around Kenna's spine as Carmen choked back tears that sprang out of nowhere. "I just want to see him happy before ..." She gritted her teeth. "Fuck, never mind."

Goosebumps rose on her arms. Nothing had ever frightened Kenna more than that pause. What was it that Carmen knew?

6

BARGAINING

Kenna

Saturday evening, Kenna stood at the sink looping twine around a bundle of white roses. Her finger caught on a thorn and a red dot swelled on its tip. She sucked the blood away without a thought, making quick work of tying off the twine.

The aching soles of her feet were a testament to her tiresome day. Carmen had dragged her to this place and that, scouting out venues, catering, and the like. With the semester officially over, and most of the wedding preparations taken care of, she was eager to relax.

Scooping up the roses, she carried them to the bathroom, where she strung them upside down from the tension rod. Earlier, Kenna expressed that she wished to have dead flowers for her bridal bouquet and Carmen had ensured her—after consulting the internet—this was the best method of preservation.

She stared at the flowers. Their full white petals. Those beautiful blooms, hung by a noose, waiting for death.

Footsteps in the other room suggested one of the twins had

come home. Rounding the corner out of the bedroom, she saw Dayton unlacing his dress shoes and, for a brief moment, she contemplated sitting next to him, kissing his cheek, offering him a warm embrace. Maybe she would have, if everything between them weren't so fucked.

Was this what domestic life was like? Welcoming your partner home after a trying day. Lighting up at the sight of their face. She hadn't welcomed him when he came through the door but a tiny thrum had vibrated within her. The pluck of a guitar string.

Suspended reverberation.

"Where's Carmen?"

The question popped the bubble surrounding Kenna's senses. Truthfully, she'd been far too fixated on his dextrous fingers unraveling the laces to pay any mind to what he'd said.

"What?"

"Carmen. Where is she?"

"Roth's. She insisted on making dinner."

"I hope you have takeout on speed dial. You witnessed her baking skills firsthand. My sister's a shit cook."

It was humanizing hearing him talk about his family, the warmth and familiarity seeping into his tone. Even if his comments were disparaging.

Dayton draped his arms over the top of the couch. He crooked a finger and Kenna beckoned forth like a lamb yielding to a shepherd's hook. Though she left a considerable distance between them, her desire to go untouched went up in smoke as his hand dove into her hair.

"She's kept you awfully busy. Did you two find a venue?"

"We did. I felt a little guilty, though. She'd researched all of these beautiful churches but, in the end, I wanted something less," she drew a sharp intake of breath as his nails grazed her scalp, "traditional."

A sound of assent rumbled low in his throat. "And where might this non-traditional setting be?"

"I want it to be a surprise. If that's alright."

"If that's alright? I'm delighted you're participating in the planning. I was sure you'd have no interest in it."

I *do* love you, she almost said. But she'd never once uttered the words and she wasn't about to debut them as a sarcastic comeback.

His fingers fled her hair, traveling south to knead her neck with his thumb and forefinger. Involuntarily, her eyebrows drew together, lips parting.

Hot breath torched the shell of her ear. "The face you're making right now? It's the same way you look when I make you come."

Her eyes flew open and she met his heated gaze. Kenna felt a flush spreading across her chest, creeping up her neck and onto her face.

"How can you do this to me?"

"Do what?" Dayton inquired, dark lashes aflutter.

"I adore you, yet I despise you. I admire you, yet I fear you. I ache for you, yet I …"

Kissing her ear, he dragged his lips along her cheek until they ghosted across her own. "There's a word for that, darling. The four-letter word you refuse to say." His voice dropped to a whisper. "But that's alright. I know you feel it. That's enough for me."

Dayton

Whether Kenna wanted to kiss him or was simply overcome with desire, he welcomed the press of her lips all the same. Dayton wanted nothing more than to pin her to the rug below and communicate exactly how much he'd missed her since they'd parted ways that morning.

But no sooner than he tasted her cloyingly sweet tongue, Carmen barged in through the front door and dismantled the romantic scene. He and Kenna pulled apart at the sound of her voice.

"Come on guys, save the Hallmark kisses for the wedding." Carmen shielded her eyes and feigned apology as she set groceries in the kitchen, but he knew his sister better than that. If anything, she was amused.

He felt like he was in high school again, calling to mind the far too many occasions on which she'd caught him with some nameless girl, pants bunched around his ankles.

"You could ring the bell. Knock, at the very least."

"Why should I? I'm a *guest*, brother."

"Just have some courtesy."

She rushed around the kitchen, figuring out where everything was supposed to go as she went. "I'm leaving in a few days. You'll soon have full range of your fuck-pad. But provoke me again, and there will be no dinner."

"In other words, I should provoke you to spare us all from food poisoning."

Loaf of bread in hand, she came into view, staring him down with a disbelieving smile. "Dayton Edward Merino. You are a piece of shit. A piece of shit that I am forced through the bonds of nature to love."

Once she was back in the kitchen and out of earshot, Dayton leaned into Kenna, whispering, "We should probably keep an eye on her so she doesn't set the house on fire."

Kenna gave a small though amused smile. Together, they abandoned the couch and joined Carmen in the kitchen. He tried to create the illusion that they were there to socialize rather than avoiding a call to the Branch Spring Fire Department. Dayton retrieved three wild ales out of the fridge. He twisted off the caps with his bare hand and passed them out.

The three of them had no trouble keeping up a friendly dialogue even before the alcohol kicked in. Most of what was said pertained to the wedding. While Kenna didn't emanate the zeal of a typical bride, she wasn't averse to the discussion and that filled him with a bit of hope.

Once the food was ready, everyone made their plates and carried them to the living room. His dining table only accommodated two and so they all sat crisscross on the floor, huddled around the coffee table. Thankfully, Carmen hadn't been too adventurous with her cooking. She'd made Cuban sandwiches.

Kenna bit into hers and a brilliant streak of mustard smeared itself next to her mouth. Dayton discretely signaled that she had something on her face. Instead of reaching for a napkin, she swiped it away with her finger and popped it into her mouth. It warmed him that she was comfortable enough to do such a thing not only in front of him, but his sister as well.

"So," Carmen began, glancing between them, "Kenna knows my secret."

"That you were adopted?" Dayton teased.

"Fuck you."

He, of course, knew exactly what she meant. In their home down in Eugene, her sexuality had been the unaddressed elephant in the room for the last 20 years of visits, holidays, and other get-togethers. He found it bittersweet that Carmen had no problem letting the world see her for who she was, but the fear of rejection made her a shell of herself around their parents.

Kenna spoke up. "I really think you should invite—sorry, what did you say her name was?"

"I didn't. It's Gia."

"You should invite Gia as your date to the wedding."

"I'd bring her in a heartbeat if our parents weren't going to be there."

Dayton found himself wondering if Kenna had grown up with any awareness of or exposure to the LGBTQ+ community. Close-knit, rural, religious, big-family farm? Probably not. It pleased him that she was trying to include Carmen in that way, even though he knew his sister would never indulge her. Not when their parents were involved. Eddy and Gwen hated shrinks and anyone who strayed from the realm of heteronormative.

Somehow, they'd birthed a set of twins who ticked both of those boxes.

They had a wonderful evening filled with conversation and, surprisingly, laughter. Carmen regaled Kenna with one too many stories from their youth and she adored them all. One of the anecdotes involved a VCR and he was surprised Kenna was familiar with the technological relic. She explained that they'd never had one in their home but they used it to watch tapes during youth Bible study. Carmen made a funny face at this. While she knew Kenna had grown up on a farm, she knew nothing else about her upbringing. The near Amish-ness of it all.

Dayton felt strange keeping that bit of knowledge from his sister. They'd told each other everything all their lives. But Kenna would soon be his wife. Her secrets were not his to tell.

Later on, they bid Carmen good night and retired to the bedroom. What he found innocently resting on his nightstand broke the pleasant spell of the last few hours. He picked up the brochure, showing it to Kenna wordlessly.

Sex and Love Addicts Anonymous was printed in bold, blue font on the front of the brochure.

She struggled to maintain eye contact as she turned down the sheets. "I printed it for you. They have a chapter in Portland. That's not too far of a drive."

"I think our sex life is more than satisfactory."

"It isn't about our sex life." Pinning her arms across her stomach, she hesitated. "It's about your history."

He raised the brochure a little higher. "This won't help me."

Her arms fell to her sides. "How do you know that?"

"Because, for a while, I went to these meetings."

"Before or after you slept with a quarter of a sorority?"

A laugh died in his throat. "It's funny. You're such a good little investigator. Good instincts. So keen. Yet you don't see it."

"What are you—"

"What is this about, exactly?" Dayton slapped the paper onto the nightstand and, though it hardly made a sound, she flinched. "You've put on a convincing act but I know you don't care how this marriage shakes out, so why are you bringing me this?"

Silence filled the room with a stifling sort of dread. He'd been harsh with her and yet he didn't apologize. A part of him wanted to but what good would it have done?

Kenna sank to the mattress. She stared pensively at the wall and when she turned her focus onto him, her voice and face both exuded an air of calm. "Because whatever happens between us after we stand at that altar, I'll always care about you. I can't turn it off."

Her truth sliced at him like a hot knife and he stood there with his melting flesh, gazing upon the woman he didn't deserve. The woman he'd deceived. He'd left bruises on her skin, her heart, and still she was brave enough to crawl into his bed every night.

He joined her beneath the sheets and killed the light, looking at the ceiling as despair grew within him like an invasive plant.

"I do think it's best you do *something* to get yourself on a more positive track," Kenna mumbled into the darkness. "When you went to Mass with me ... well, I really enjoyed that. It's not a support group and it isn't therapy, but I think you could benefit from it. Nathan and his wife are always there." As a final appeal, she added, "Would you agree to that? Mass, every Sunday?"

"If you start running with me."

7

NEW LIFE

Kenna

*K*enna looked on in deep admiration as Mr. Walden tried feebly to answer a series of questions posed by Dayton.

The elderly man was retired and had lost his wife a few years earlier. In her absence, he'd developed a severe case of agoraphobia. He and his wife had done everything together, and when she passed he became terrified of his usual routines: grocery shopping, medical appointments, and the like.

He feared anything that drew him out of the quaint home he'd shared with his wife for 45 years and into the world at large. It was really quite a sweet story, however sad it may have been. Her relationship with Dayton was quickly approaching the same territory. If one of them were to leave, by death or some other force, would the other be able to carry on?

Not because of their love, but rather this vicious dependency they had on one another. This deep-rooted connection they could not shake.

Fighting to clear her head, Kenna shifted in her seat.

For months, Dayton had conducted his psychotherapy sessions with Mr. Walden via video chat. All those hours of remote therapy had paid off. It was truly a marvel to see him there, sitting on the velvet chaise, timidly yet proudly embracing his new normal.

When the hour expired, they saw Mr. Walden out and made sure he knew the date of his next appointment. Carmen had borrowed a chair from Dayton's private office and set up shop alongside Kenna at the reception desk, though he'd implored her not to touch anything.

"You got a call."

Dayton regarded her, unamused. "I thought I made it clear you were not to answer the phone."

"It was your friend, dipshit." She rolled her eyes like a disgruntled elementary schooler. "He called the office line because you weren't answering your cell."

"Well, of course not. I was with a patient. Did he leave a message?"

Carmen shrugged. "Code blue?"

For a beat, Dayton turned gravely serious and it gave Kenna half a fright. "You're sure that's what he said?"

"Yes, but what does it—"

He leaned over the reception desk, completely infringing on his sister's personal space, and shut the computer down. "We have to go to the hospital."

The women watched, perplexed, as Dayton flicked lights off here and there, moving with great purpose. He disappeared through the hall.

"Why?" Carmen shouted, loud enough to ensure she was heard. "What the hell is going on?"

Practically flying around the corner, he pushed on the front door, looking back at them with his face half-bathed in daylight. "They're having their baby."

. . .

A birth in a hospital. It was something that had long been normalized. Of course, her family had done things their way. As a young girl, Kenna remembered being too afraid to peek inside the room, the bloodied towels and feral cries from her mother. And then, when she was older, she helped with the birth of her youngest sister, Oona. She boiled water and sponged her mother's forehead and looked on in horror as her new sibling emerged, glazed in life's essence.

The memories flicked through her head as she sat in the waiting room with Carmen. The Scotts' baby was born shortly before the trio made it to the hospital. Dayton and Nathan were at the store picking up a few forgotten items for their stay.

Carmen stretched her legs out, elbows planted on the poorly cushioned arms of the chair. "This is way more excitement than I signed up for."

"I only found out recently that they were expecting. Did you know?" Kenna prompted.

"Nope. But it's not all that surprising." Before Kenna could get a word in, Carmen was changing the subject. "So, how do you feel about not having kids?"

She shouldn't have been thrown by the question and yet everything was off-balance. She licked her lips. Swallowed. Blinked. She could only stall for so long before she was forced to accept the greater implication behind what Carmen had said. Her curiosity, her investigation, had led her down a path that ended with marriage and all that came with it.

At least, she prayed that's where it ended.

"I've had time to think about it, and I don't feel any differently about being with him. He made the choice before we met."

Carmen gave a single nod and, for a stretch of what became uncomfortable silence, she studied the toes of her shoes. Until her eyes snapped up to Kenna and she said something that threatened to send the younger woman to the emergency room. The psych ward. Anywhere to escape her own mind.

"It was a tough decision for him, you know? Just about killed him. He always wanted a family."

The words caused a glitch in her brain. Like malware, it infected everything. Tainted whatever she thought she knew and made her question things that she'd been convinced were settled.

The issue of Erin Wright reopened.

Further analysis was obviously necessary.

Across the way, the entrance's automatic doors parted with a whisper and two familiar men came through, one of whom she recognized less and less every day.

Dayton

He'd known, by virtue of prior experience, that leaving Kenna with Carmen was ill-advised. And Dayton had done so again with total disregard, though he'd argue that he had no choice. Nathan had dragged him out of Owens-Adair before he'd been able to protest.

It felt like Purgatory, that agonizing limbo, as the powers of Paradiso and the Inferno silently looked on, forming their judgments. But this was a hospital waiting room and his sister and fiancée did not wield the power of God. Even if it seemed that way, with flames licking his ankles as he spoke to Carmen, and peered every so often at Kenna, who was quiet and out of reach but radiant in her presence. That golden light, that guiding force. Dayton wouldn't disappoint her.

Yet he suspected the damage was done.

Was it nothing more than premature animosity toward her soon-to-be sister-in-law? Who was he kidding? The two of them got along splendidly.

Carmen had betrayed him, then. She'd gone and shot her mouth off one too many times when he wasn't around, poisoning his fiancée's mind with the truth. Except his sister would sooner off herself than double-cross him.

His thoughts started to calm. Perhaps Carmen hadn't said anything explicit, but even if she'd said something veiled in vague language, it worried him. Kenna's ability to intuit was incredible.

Dayton thought of how very strange it was to be in the lobby. It wasn't a Friday night at the E.R. He wasn't there to check on a patient from the practice who'd ended up on the 7th floor for any multitude of reasons—none of which was ever good. He wasn't laid up in the C.C.U.

Tonight, he was merely a visitor. He was there to celebrate a happy occasion. Faintly, he smiled to himself.

He could do with more happiness.

Kenna

The sun had long since set beyond the hospital's walls. She and Carmen had pilfered the vending machine and scraped together a pitiful dinner, and they'd all drunk far too much of the sludge the lobby attendants were passing off as coffee. Kenna was beginning to wonder if they were going to have to configure some sort of sleeping arrangement in the waiting area when Professor Scott finally approached from the direction of the elevators.

"The little man is accepting visitors."

"Congratulations." Dayton rose and pulled him in for a hug that stunned everyone. When they parted, he patted his friend's back. "Hey, you better do an exemplary job raising him or he'll end up in my office one day."

He shook his head. "My son's not even three hours old and you're already trying to psychoanalyze him."

Slinging an arm around his shoulder, Dayton said, "Come on, Nathaniel, that's why we're such good friends. We grind each other's gears."

The four of them piled into the elevator and rode it up to the maternity ward. Knots formed in Kenna's stomach, but she didn't know why. She had no reason to be nervous. She didn't know the Scotts terribly well, and there was the constant reminder that Nathan was her former professor. Even if the situation was made logical by her association with Dayton, it still felt strange that she was moments away from meeting their child.

Walking down that hallway, Kenna felt young, inexperienced, and out of place, when in reality she was none of those things.

They all crept as quietly as they could into the room, standing to form a semicircle at the foot of Charlaine's bed. Her exhaustion was palpable. Pallor had claimed the natural radiance of her skin and her eyelids were half shut.

"How are you feeling?" Kenna asked.

Charlaine let out a big breath. "Tired."

The baby laid beside the bed in a rollaway bassinet. Swaddled and capped, he slowly wriggled about. A caterpillar in its cocoon. A paper suctioned to the inside of the acrylic declared his name, weight, time of birth, and other relevant details.

Professor Scott looked between his wife and Dayton. "Do you want to deliver the news?"

Arching a brow, Charlaine said, "I think I've done more than my fair share of delivering."

Soft laughter rippled through the room.

"We want you to be Isaiah's godfather."

Carmen's hand flew to her mouth and she ran out into the hall. The Scotts may have found the reaction strange but Kenna now understood perfectly well.

He would never have a son of his own.

Dayton's eyes darted here and there, as if he wasn't sure where to focus his attention. He pointed to himself. "Me? After what I did at your wedding?"

"Water under the bridge," Professor Scott said.

"Besides," Charlaine interjected, "you two were friends before I came along."

Dayton didn't verbally accept or decline the honor that had

been foisted on him, but soon Professor Scott was scooping his son out of the bassinet and delicately handing him over.

The beauty of what followed was unexpected.

Every dark part of him stripped away as he held the innocent life in his arms. To Kenna, he became unrecognizable. Everything she thought she knew about him begged new questions. For the first time, she didn't feel the need to seek answers.

Silently, she beheld Dayton as he tucked the newborn close to his chest, a faint hint of joy flickering over his austere face.

June

8

RUN FROM ME

Dayton

That familiar, sweet fire singed his lungs as he jogged along the trail. He preferred to move faster, but he slowed his usual pace to accommodate Kenna.

She hardly kept up, frequently folding in half and calling out after him. She'd stayed close during the 5K and he'd bordered on an actual run then. Though, at that time, her movement was probably fueled by pure spite.

Dayton came to a stop. Stretching his arms overhead, he watched as Kenna walk-jogged from about a hundred yards away.

They were on a trail not too far from downtown East Haven. He had discovered it one morning on his commute to the practice, thanks to some clearly marked signage, and ran it later that evening. He'd been coming to the trail for months. Sometimes twice a day.

Running cleansed him—but only as long as the run lasted. Then his vicious cycle of thoughts began anew.

Kenna's face came into focus as she neared and all that worried him temporarily faded away. He glanced at her hand. She'd left her engagement ring at home. It hurt, seeing her bare finger, but whether she wore it or not, he knew she was fully committed to their little plan.

Smoothing her flyaways back, she breathed harshly, "I don't suppose we could've started on Fairbrook?"

"I avoid town. Unless I'm running at night."

She seemed genuinely intrigued by this. "Why?"

He shrugged. "The woods aren't exactly conducive for a run once the sun sets. I sure as hell wouldn't attempt it even with a miner's hat." This earned him a laugh. That feathery, lyrical sound he adored. He scanned their surroundings for effect. "Who knows what's out there. Wolves, mountain lions, bears."

"I think I'm in capable hands. Although, I'd argue that you're just as dangerous."

"You think so?"

"Fairly confident."

Maybe his villainous act was useless. Maybe she saw straight through him. Oh, to have been a fly on the wall during one of her and Carmen's many conversations.

His sister was in need of a stern talking to.

Kenna vacuumed in the humid air. He felt guilty for not bringing along water. His brows knitted together in concern. "Can you make it the rest of the way?"

"I'll manage. You're not stepping out halfway through Mass and I'm not going to give you a reason to."

Then she did something that took him by surprise. She raised up on her tiptoes and kissed his scarred cheek. It was rare for Kenna to offer up any kind of affection. Usually anything intimate that transpired between them was his doing.

Dayton smiled at her, and for one perfect moment, she became the beautiful flower she'd been at Purgatory, leaning toward his synthetic light.

Kenna

Kenna was rather pleased with herself as she got ready for Mass that evening. Never in her wildest dreams would she have believed Dayton could be bargained with. She knew it was foolish, striking a compromise on any scale with a man like him.

The devil always stakes his claim.

She practically turned the bedroom upside down searching for her wooden St. Rose bracelet. It had been a couple of days since she'd last worn it but it wasn't in any of its usual resting places. Considering the size of the house, it was a wonder anything managed to go missing.

"Dayton?" Kenna called, absentmindedly wringing her empty wrist. "Have you seen my bracelet?"

"Can't quite hear you."

Sighing, she retreated to the other room. His fingers performed a quick dance on the keyboard and his laptop grayed out. It was an annoying trick he'd recently employed, hiding his screen whenever she came around. This, of course, grated her nerves to no end.

He treated that laptop as if it were a borrowed artifact from some high-brow museum. As soon as Kenna went to sleep, he glued himself to it, evidenced by the many nights she'd awoken to relentless keyboard clacking. During the day, the computer remained in its case. Tucked away. Safe.

Dayton smiled. Sugar and venom. "Darling, I'd prefer it if you didn't shout across the house."

She ran her tongue along the inside of her teeth. The many biting comebacks that filled her head stayed there, fearing their deliverance would result in him going back on his promise.

"My bracelet. I've looked all over and I can't find it. Have you seen it?"

He put an elbow on the desk, thumb placed thoughtfully on his chin. "Remind me again what it looks like."

A silent assertion stood between them. No matter how many

compromises were reached, or vows were said, or love was made, he was still in control.

And that subtly antagonizing comment, along with the spark in his eye, was his way of reminding her.

Kenna wouldn't let him rile her. She'd paid her dues in the woods that morning. "Forget I mentioned it. We should get going."

More and more, she found herself thinking of the email to the Oregon Medical Board that she hadn't had the courage to send. Would it have stopped any of this? Would Lacey have been ... No. She couldn't think about that.

Dayton put on his shoes and straightened his clothes and, in him, she saw everything her parents had spent 18 years warning her about.

According to them, hands were for three things: working, helping, and praying. She'd gone and dirtied hers. Tainted them in a way that they'd never come clean. Kenna's heart lurched. Did God even hear her prayers anymore? Or were they muffled by sin? Rendered inaudible.

She didn't notice the lone tear skidding along her cheek until Dayton wiped it away.

"If the bracelet means that much to you, I'll help you look for it tonight."

She wanted to believe the concern etched into his features if only to make the life she led easier. Kenna gave a slight nod, a wordless gesture of acceptance, and soon they were out the door.

As promised, Dayton helped her search their home top to bottom once they'd returned from Mass. He even pulled up the floorboards and let her check his hidey-hole; though she had a sneaking suspicion it was solely to save face.

Kenna collapsed onto the couch. She stared at the ceiling's wooden beams, feeling defeated. Paranoid. Had she misplaced it or had he taken it? If he had, what purpose did it serve? She tried to push the thought aside but the missing bracelet gave way to the missing, murdered girl and, like a switch had engaged in her brain, she mentally ran through her database of information.

Something made her think of Audrey. The sorority, all those girls. Lacey had been in a sorority. But so what? Kenna was grasping at straws and she knew it. Yet a yanking sensation in her gut insisted she needed to make a phone call.

She'd never been more thankful to be menstruating.

Heavy footsteps creaked on the hardwood and her hand shot to her lower abdomen, willing herself to dramatize the minor pain she felt. Dayton perched on the edge of the couch, frowning.

"Cramps?"

She nodded, hoping her lack of verbal response was a testament to her contrived discomfort.

He rose at once. Pocketing his keys, he said, "I'll pick up something for the pain. Is there anything else you need?"

Dayton beheld her with the moonstruck gaze of a devoted husband. Her heart might have softened a bit if she wasn't eager to shove him out the door.

While she had been confident the plan would work, she was relieved after he'd left the driveway. The house was free of any and all kinds of medication—thanks to his cardio issues. Kenna had been blessed with unusually light cramps. She'd never needed medicine for them. But Dayton didn't have to know that.

Audrey hadn't given her a phone number, so she settled for a video call over social media. Loud ringing filled the house as her insides flip-flopped. The screen was dark but Audrey was visible due to the scarce halo of light radiating from her phone.

"Kenna?"

"Sorry to bother you."

"It's no bother at all." She lowered her voice. "Everything okay?"

There was no shortage of things Kenna could've said, 'no' being the most obvious and concise. "There's something I want to ask you."

"Sure."

"Don't read into this too much, I'm just curious. Did anyone go missing at UCLA while you two were together? Anyone from your sorority, maybe?"

"Oh my God. That dead girl. Lacey something."

"How do you know about that?"

"Are you serious? They're turning the country upside down looking for the killer. It's national news."

National. Kenna let it all sink in. Shane Sanders was being hunted like a prized buck and every household in America was keeping tabs. Sanders could've been the one responsible. But too many 'what ifs' had let loose in her brain, the most terrifying of which she shared a bed with.

"You don't … you don't think Dayton had anything to do with this, do you?" Audrey asked.

The truth she'd safeguarded like a nuclear warhead eked past her lips. "Maybe."

Well past midnight, once Dayton was sound asleep, she quietly snuck onto the front porch, laptop clutched to her chest. The night was calming. The still, serene street and the breeze whispering through the trees. A tabby cat ran out of the azaleas and gave her a fright as she settled on the top step.

She queued up news coverage of the manhunt. Her stomach turned upon seeing a familiar face in many of the thumbnails.

Detective Reynolds' unflinching gaze locked onto her. Even though they were separated by time and distance, it was just as intimidating as when he'd sat across from her in the diner.

She drew back. The corner of his mouth twitched in time with her slamming the laptop shut.

9

FRAGILE

Dayton

"I don't want you to see it on the hanger. It'll spoil tomorrow."

Dayton played along with Kenna's request and turned his back as she stuffed the gown into the trunk. He didn't turn around until it closed.

Something genuine backlit her eyes. It was a rare, giddy moment between them. The evidence stood five feet away and still he could not believe it.

She was looking forward to tomorrow.

Contentment hummed through his veins as he drove her to the other side of town. They'd decided to go the traditional route of sleeping separately the night before the wedding. Kenna was staying at a rental with his mother and sister while he and his father took the house.

Magnificent beauty surrounded them on all sides. Lush trees. Blossoming flowers. Spring morphed into summer, where that greenery would flourish until it fell into fall's clutches. His grip tightened on the wheel. Was that all he and Kenna had?

One glorious, blissful summer until the decay set in, whatever form it took.

Her withdrawal. His arrest. Ghosts of subjects past coming out of the woodwork to further drive a wedge between them.

It was what he deserved. What he had coming.

Dayton's hand splayed across his chest as a violent pain shot through it. Were he being honest, it was much more than painful. It was nauseating. Fingernails dug into his heart and punctured its tissue. Clawing. Squeezing.

Pulling over into a bank of grass, he cut off the engine. He tore out of the car and harvested the fresh air, hands planting firmly on his thighs to steady himself.

The passenger door shut. Grass rustled. Kenna put a hand on the middle of his back. "Hey, what's going on? Are you alright?"

His constricted throat trapped any response. A familiar wave rolled through him and knocked him to his knees. Dayton braced his arms on the ground as the vomit spewed. Tears, born out of exertion, sprinkled the dirt.

Kenna went back to the car but quickly returned. She squatted beside him, offering a bottle of water. He poured some into his palm and scrubbed his face before downing the rest, glancing at her while he drank. A wordless thank you.

"Does that happen a lot?"

They were so completely and utterly consumed by one another that he often forgot they didn't know every niggling detail of each other's existence. She was aware of his illness, but clueless to the ways in which it affected him.

As an adolescent, Dayton had been standoffish at the idea of letting anyone get close enough to see his fatal flaw. He feared intimacy but craved it all the same.

One taste of carnal flesh had sealed his fate.

He managed a nod.

"I'm sorry you have to go through that."

Self-deprecation tugged at his lips. "This is my life." He grabbed one of her hands and held it with both of his. "I have you now. We have each other." Something softened in her expression. God, he would've taken her in the grass if he hadn't been worried about the possibility of a cop cruising by. "We're a team, you and I. I want us to help each other through anything. Big or small. Promise me that."

She stood, looking down on him, and it was as if she saw straight through him. His doubts. His fear.

"Tomorrow's for promises. If that's what you want, ask me at the altar, with God and everyone else as your witness."

Without asking, she got into the driver's side of the car and waited for him to follow suit.

Kenna

Kenna was exceptionally nervous to spend the night in a foreign house with Carmen and Gwen, though she regarded the former fondly. Gwen had been cordial enough during last year's holiday ambush, but Kenna worried she wouldn't be as kind in her son's absence.

Her overnight bag dropped to the floor with a *thunk* and she was embraced by a crushing set of arms that she instantly recognized as Carmen's. After a minute, they separated.

Her face split into a toothy grin. "Are you freaking out yet?"

"Pretty calm, actually," Kenna said. "So, no Gia?"

Even though she had lowered her voice to ask the question, Carmen gently shut the bedroom door. She slumped onto the corner of the bed and the box spring emitted a high-pitched squeak.

"I'd absolutely kill to share these moments with her but, at the end of the day, I just couldn't do it."

"Why?"

"Because I'd never forgive myself if I ruined my brother's wedding."

Another squeak emerged as Kenna sat on the opposite corner. She studied Carmen's tattoo sleeve up close for the first time. Felicity and Perpetua were the focal point of the piece, set against stained glass. Kenna found the inclusion of the glass rather odd, as the piece was done in grayscale. Why include something beautiful when the thing that made it so—the color—was absent?

Her criticism was soon forgotten as she registered the significance of the saints. They were apostasies who refused to forsake their own beliefs and conform to the religion of the people. Kenna wondered if the tattoo had less to do with Carmen's Catholic upbringing and more to do with the fact that those women inked onto her skin were a perfect representation of her struggle with identity and acceptance in the face of those she loved. In that way, the grayscale made sense. It placed a somber veil over the scene.

"Are you going to keep her a secret forever?" It came off as innocent enough and Carmen displayed no offense.

"I've thought about telling my dad. He might take it okay. It isn't that I hate my mom, I just think she has it in her head that Dayton and I are these little chess pieces she can move across a board and if we don't make the moves she wants, she loses interest in playing. Kind of always how it's been."

What else had Dayton inherited from his mother besides her dark, lifeless eyes? Sadistic satisfaction from manipulating those around him?

Maybe that's all their relationship was. Him getting off on the knowledge that he had every ounce of control over her.

No.

This wasn't a one-sided game. They were both playing. She only hoped that, at last, they were on the same team rather than opponents.

Kenna felt the need to say something as Carmen advanced toward the door, her hand already reaching for the knob.

"I'm always here if you need to talk. In a more casual capacity, of course. I won't be licensed until graduation next spring."

"Thank you," she said. Carmen gave her a look that one might employ when gazing upon someone who had it far worse. Kenna's spine went rigid, as if it had been replaced by a solid plank. "That's very kind."

Kenna couldn't sleep. She had told Carmen that she was calm but once the sun set anxiety gripped her. What was there to be nervous about?

They were already married on paper.

A few days after the proposal, they had gone to city hall and made it official in the government's eyes. She had complained about her nonexistent insurance and Dayton had suggested that they should 'go ahead and get it over with' so she could have adequate medical coverage.

Signing the documents weeks ahead of the wedding didn't faze her. She was marrying him to ensure she wasn't used as a check-mate in the event of a murder trial. She couldn't imagine what might have happened between now and 'I do' that would surpass that on the disbelief scale.

The floorboards didn't creak like they did at home—*home*, she was still getting used to saying it—and so it was seamless sneaking into the kitchen without disturbing anyone.

Not bothering to turn on the light, Kenna rummaged through the cabinets, softly closing each one, in search of tea or anything else that might settle her nerves. She wasn't a big proponent of liquor, but she was desperate enough to down the fiery liquid if it meant a good night's rest.

"Trouble sleeping?"

Were the scene not terribly familiar, she would've jumped at the voice. Light flooded the space and revealed Gwen stationed at the table, a steaming mug before her. She looked every bit the villainous mother-in-law with her close-cropped chic haircut, silk robe, and silently disapproving stare.

"Yes."

Gwen nodded to an empty chair and Kenna filled it without hesitation. She sat there, beside Dayton's gracefully aging mother, and convinced herself that she had lost her foothold in reality and all of this was taking place in an alternate dimension. A dreamscape. That was it. This was a dream. She'd never left her bed. She was still sound asleep.

Kenna would've believed the lie had it not been for the many things pointing to her lucidity. The harsh white overhead light. The cardamom of Gwen's perfume hitting her with the force of smelling salts. Simultaneous sweat and chills assaulted Kenna as she sat frozen at that kitchen table.

"All of this is quite," she struggled to find the appropriate word, "sudden."

"I happen to agree."

"We've met you on one occasion, for God's sake."

The question Kenna anticipated—*what's the hurry?*—did not come.

"Is he happy?" A note of tender desperation broke through her level tone.

"Honestly? It's hard to tell." She thought for a moment, adding for Gwen's sake, "But we're in love, and that love is filled with an understanding and appreciation of each other's every part, every fissure, every flaw."

Cheeks heating, she stared at the tabletop.

"Flaw," Gwen repeated. The smile that brightened her face made Kenna uneasy. "You know."

Vagueness had never been so blood-curdling.

When she didn't respond, Gwen continued, "You're aware of his … conditions."

The *s* slithered through her mind's garden. Had she missed something? Surely, she wasn't about to get a revelatory, diagnostic bomb from a woman who rejected psychiatry outright.

"We've been incredibly fortunate. I thank God every day that I was able to raise him, to see him grow up, become an adult, and now, to see him get married? There was a time I never thought any of that would be my reality."

"He was hospitalized. Last winter. Did you know?"

She laid the truth down like a winning card in a poker game, as if it implied she was of greater importance to Dayton than his own mother. As if to say, *he may have crawled into the world from between your legs but it is between mine he hides from it.* The thought was wildly unlike her, and Kenna wondered where it came from. This was a vulnerable conversation, not a pissing contest.

Gwen shook her head.

"We used to hear from him all the time. He'd visit when he was able. But, over the last couple of years, he's become so distant." Her chin trembled but she quickly steadied. "I don't think it was God's will for Dayton to live. Why else would he have tried to end a life so young, hardly begun? He fought, though. He did. Two conflicting heart abnormalities. He was sick all the time as a child. We couldn't give him antibiotics like we could with Carmen. It was a lot to endure as a mother, watching your child go through that and wondering why God had made him more fragile than everyone else."

She looked at Gwen and no longer saw a terrifying matriarch, but a mother who feared for her son. Seeing that new side of her gave Kenna the courage to speak up.

"I've studied alongside him for a year and a half. His work means everything to him. I know you're averse to what he does. You're his mother." She paused. "You asked me earlier if he was happy. His real happiness lies in his career."

Gwen nodded slowly, as if she were digesting the idea.

"Perhaps it's best if you don't get too attached." She rose, depositing her mug in the sink, and turned to face Kenna with a sobering expression. "Any day could be his last."

She swept out of the room and Kenna was left alone in the bright, cold kitchen, tied down to the chair with the weight of Gwen's warning.

SWEET NOTHINGS

Kenna

*W*ere she ever to get married, Kenna had long pictured the New York countryside as the backdrop.

Never in her wildest dreams did she think she'd wind up in the Pacific Northwest, saying 'I do' amid the breathtaking network of pines. They had yet to leave the rental but Kenna could already smell their sweet vanilla musk, that signature fragrance. Everything she associated with it skittered through her mind's eye like a film reel—all of which linked to Dayton.

She studied her reflection in the vintage dressing mirror, certain she had never looked this beautiful while also knowing that beauty would not be surpassed by any future occasion, however distant.

The gown fit the same as when she'd tried it on in the shop a few weeks before. Instead of heels, Kenna had opted for white ballet shoes. Growing up, she had always wondered what the dainty shoes would feel like on her feet and she marveled over their comfort as she stood there before the mirror. She didn't mind that the fabric pooling at the bottom of the dress obscured her footwear.

The shoes were just for her. They represented a sliver of control amid this situation she had been thrust into.

Kenna startled as a knock came against the doorframe. Carmen wore a jade green cocktail dress, keys and phone in one hand. "All set?"

"I think so."

"You look amazing, really." Her head angled in admiration.

She wanted to say 'thank you,' but the words got all tangled in her throat. Stuck. Kenna tried to smile though she felt no movement in her facial muscles.

Before she turned to leave, she gave her reflection a wistful glance. It was ironic, dressing like a princess on the day she'd lose her freedom.

Dayton

His heart sang with delight as he and his father arrived at the venue Kenna had managed to keep a secret through all their weeks of preparation.

With great deliberation, Dayton got out of the car and stood facing the wall of trees. He didn't smile or say anything to his father. Instead, he looked on, a strange mix of solemnity and pure joy in his gut. His vision blurred. Something splattered on his jacket. Wiping at his eyes, he pulled his fingers away and examined them, noting how they glistened.

Seldom did he cry as an emotional response.

So often, his tears were harvested, his illness' way of making him pay tithe for every breath he took, every second he remained alive.

It was, perhaps, a great shame that Dayton didn't gain a full appreciation for his life until that moment.

He looked over at his father and found a weathered shadow of the strong, intelligent man who'd raised him. Silently, he vowed to spend more time with him, with his mother, with Carmen. He would. His marriage to Kenna, sham or not, would make him a better man. Repair all that was broken within him.

"Have any last-minute advice?" Dayton asked.

"Just love her, son. But love is easy." Stuffing his hands in his pockets, Eddy glanced at him. "It's everything that comes with it that's hard."

Pines towered above them as they walked along the trail. He studied their many branches, each of them unique. Some were thick and some were thin. Some were curved and others were straight. Their needles formed fine green points. Youthful pine cones accented the greenery.

Beautiful, simplistic innocence.

Kenna had embodied that before he'd come along.

He was the blight, that man-made corruption that poisoned everything it touched.

Midway through, the trail opened up into a clearing. The ceremony space occupied one side and the tented area for the reception was on the other. His father went off in search of his mother. What few guests were invited started arriving.

Dayton walked along the perimeter of the scene, admiring everything from a distance. It warmed his cold heart that the very location in which Kenna had saved his life would be the place where they joined theirs.

Leaning against a tree, he took in the sight. His family, acquaintances, former colleagues. The formality and significance of it all.

His hand slipped into his pocket and absentmindedly fondled the box that housed their wedding bands.

"Dayton."

The whisper was so faint, he thought he'd imagined it. Then he realized the sound arose from behind the tree.

He kept his focus forward, speaking at a comparable volume.

"Kenna? I thought, according to you, we weren't supposed to see or speak to each other before the ceremony."

"We aren't, but this can't wait."

The bottom of his stomach fell away and he felt as if he were trapped in a rising elevator with a broken panic button. There was a very narrow possibility that whatever she had to say was positive.

"Go on."

"I know everything." He nearly lunged around the tree and put his forearm to her neck until she tacked on, "About your heart conditions. I'm sure you had your reasons for keeping me in the dark, but I just wanted to say that I'm here for you, and I want to support you in whatever way you'll allow. I—"

She went quiet for a moment. His heart thundered in his chest and his breath suspended in anticipation of her words.

"We can get through this together. Everything else, too, because the truth is, Dayton, I love you. I do."

The corners of his mouth raised slightly. He reached his hand around the tree and she grasped it for a moment before letting go.

11

DEAD SILENCE

Kenna

Florence Welch's rendition of 'Stand By Me' belted from a portable speaker as Eddy, arm locked with hers, guided her slowly along the aisle.

Their song choice was horribly fitting.

Kenna had mostly agreed to marry Dayton on the off chance he had killed someone and the even slighter chance she wouldn't have to testify against him if he was arrested and stood trial. How romantic.

And yet there *was* something romantic about being there, walking down an aisle of twigs and earth in the woods where she had played a small role in saving Dayton's life.

She was dressed in a pool of satin Vera Wang, his diamond weighing on her finger as she clutched a bouquet of garnet roses—dead, preserved—and, though she'd confessed her love to him, she wondered the very thing everyone in her position must have contemplated: Was she making a mistake?

Yes, Kenna was certain down to her marrow, but what else would she have done? What, if not marry him?

She understood with a grim fatality that if they were to part, by way of life or death, there'd be no getting over him. Any attempt to move on would be futile.

He'd haunt the gallery of her mind until the day she died, and she conceded that time would be better spent with him rather than with his memory.

Dayton stood at the metal arch shrouded in vines that served as their altar, politely clasping his hands, hair trimmed a little shorter upon Carmen's insistence. What right did he have, passing as this average guy? Getting married. She knew what lurked beneath the pristine, overly groomed exterior.

Someone who held the power to hurt and to love her in frighteningly equal measure. Someone she loved with a devotion dark and true.

He was Lucifer in a tuxedo. It's a wonder he hadn't worn her heart as a pocket square.

Beyond the chairs, a woman stood dressed in all black, as if she were attending a funeral rather than a wedding. She wore a wide-brimmed black hat and oversized sunglasses, long hair carried by the breeze. Kenna's mouth grew taut as she studied the stranger but she soon returned her focus to the altar, where the priest gave her the faintest smile before addressing Eddy.

"Do you give this woman away to this man?"

Eddy muttered something akin to consent, surrendered her arm, and took his seat in the front row alongside Gwen and Carmen.

She wished Nathan had escorted her to the altar rather than Dayton's father, but Carmen had taken the reins on the wedding planning so Kenna wasn't in a position to complain. The one thing she had insisted on was the venue—which had demanded a staggering amount of back and forth between them and the church officials before receiving a reluctant green light. For everything else, she'd employed the compliancy of a puppet.

As she joined Dayton's side, she caught a glimpse at what would've been the space reserved for her family and friends, and her stomach lurched at its emptiness.

No one had shown up for her.

She didn't blame them, but it didn't sting any less. The bonfire party had been the final nail in the coffin for the precious few half-friendships she had left. And Kenna had ignored her family for years. While she was entirely to blame for their absence, something within her ached, something that now felt foreign as it surfaced because she'd buried it for so long. She wondered, fleetingly, what her father would say were he to ever find out that someone else had brought her down the aisle.

Despite that ache, Kenna knew it was for the best that her family wasn't present. Her parents never supported her decision to attend university and she could only imagine their disgust upon learning that she'd ended up married to someone who she had once studied under. Not to mention the glaring fact that Dayton was 17 years her senior.

A light breeze swirled through the air, disturbing the curls draping over her shoulders. Kenna's pulse pounded in the cage of her chest, so loud it was impossible to decipher the priest's speech.

The unwelcome feeling of being watched crept over her. She knew everyone was, more than likely, staring at them. It was their wedding after all.

But when she glanced to her right, it was Dayton who stared at her. He didn't look out of the corner of his eye or try to be covert in any way. A full head turn. Every ounce of his focus was on Kenna and it sent her skin prickling, recalling the way he'd looked at her the night they'd first slept together. Mirroring that same reverence. His gaze, worshipful. Her heartbeat settled as the priest's words recaptured her attention.

"If anyone objects to this union, please rise."

Kenna waited for him to proceed but instead he gazed out into the crowd as a deep vertical crease formed between his gathered brows. Part of her expected to find Detective Reynolds had been the source of the objection, and that he would call out the ugly nature of their marriage in front of everyone. The detective's face flashed through her mind, recalling the unsettling way he had locked eyes with her through the laptop screen as if he'd been peering into her soul.

She heard Dayton swallow, how it seemed to cut through the air. An eerie quiet had fallen over everything. No mumbling chatter of guests or squeaks from the rental chairs as people adjusted in their seats.

Dead silence. The breeze strengthened.

An icy sensation trailed up her spine. From the growing insistence of the wind or the unease of the moment, she wasn't sure. Kenna and Dayton exchanged a glance, their faces holding thinly veiled dread as they turned in unison to face the crowd. Her chest tightened within the prison-like bodice of her dress, a feeling she thought impossible, as her eyes landed on the lone person standing beyond the seating area.

The woman in black.

Dayton

Dayton conjured his hardest look as Kenna glanced back and forth between him and Jasmine. An imperceptible shift came over her face, like an unspoken apology, before she walked away.

He scarcely managed to keep down his breakfast as she left him standing at the altar. Dayton assured the guests that everything was 'just fine' and they were taking a brief intermission.

He stood off to the side of the ceremony space, taking deep breaths that did little to calm him. He would've done anything for a joint but he'd given up marijuana months ago, finally heeding the tired advice of his former cardiologist.

Footsteps approached.

Nathan had a smug look on his face. "Let me guess, that girl was one of the many PYT's you've hit and quit?"

Dayton ran his tongue roughly along his molars. He wasn't in the mood for his friend's teasing, even if it was good-natured. Not when Kenna was preparing to dive into a conversation that would worsen her already poor perception of him.

"Something like that."

"Well, you know what they say. Karma's a bitch. After the stunt you pulled at *my* wedding?"

"I did apologize."

"You groveled. There was no official apology."

"Is this necessary? My wife just left me at the altar."

A tense moment of silence passed between them. Nathan stuffed his hands in his pockets and Dayton stared at the reception tent, where the women had wandered.

"What do you think they're talking about?"

"Oh, I have an idea," Dayton said, tracing the scar at the hollow of his throat.

1 2

IN COLD BLOOD

Kenna

How painfully full circle she'd come; fleeing the farm only to wind up on the other side of the country, living out a few blissful years before falling head over fears for a man whose sway over her was even more powerful than that of her family.

She sat across from another of his victims.

On their wedding day, no less.

Jasmine had long, straight, dark brown hair that fell to her waist. She pulled off her dark sunglasses, revealing a pair of heavy-lidded deep amber eyes that stared straight through Kenna.

She glossed over pleasantries and began with the most obvious question. "How did you know about the wedding?"

"That's all he's posted about for weeks. I hung around Dayton's house this morning," Jasmine's gaze fell to the tabletop then snapped back to her, "and I followed him here."

For whatever reason, the admission made Kenna uncomfortable. She hadn't known any of the girls to be dangerous. And while

73

she didn't yet know what Jasmine was after, stalking Dayton—as much as he deserved it—wasn't a promising sign.

"Let me guess." Kenna had no intention to be rude but saw no harm in being straightforward. "You're here to warn me. He's bad news. I should run now."

Something dimmed Jasmine's natural radiance.

"Is this a joke to you?"

"Far from it, it's just—" She hesitated. "I've heard it all before. You do know there are others, don't you?"

"Can't say that I did, but it doesn't surprise me. Has he told you anything about me?"

"Not a word."

While that was true, Kenna knew about the illicit sex tape, but that was something she'd found all on her own. A blush bloomed across her cheeks that she hoped her layers of foundation concealed.

An extended pause stretched between them. Jasmine looked at Kenna, at the table, at the interior of the tent, and back around again. She opened and closed her mouth several times.

"I don't know how else to say this." A misty veil came over her eyes as she cocked her jaw to one side. "He killed my boyfriend."

The ground shook and the seams of the earth splintered, the cold dirt enveloping Kenna and delivering her into the fiery pits of Hell.

Her rib cage felt as if it were in danger of snapping and she wanted to claw away at her dress. But she sat there, quietly composed while, inside, everything crumbled away.

"Jasmine."

"You don't believe me?" There was an icy edge to her voice. Unflinching, she slid her phone across the table. "Open it."

Kenna started to shake her head but she looked at the screen, swiping up to unlock it. Her face and limbs grew cold as she blanched at the horrific image.

It was a scene ripped straight out of a nightmare.

Mangled car parts. Dents, entire sections ripped away. Shattered glass. Blood coating the broken pieces. The limp young man in the driver's seat.

"Tyler's mom was there. She begged me not to take photos. She didn't understand why I was taking them, why I *had* to take them. But I think you do. You know what he is."

Of course she knew. She knew and she'd ignored it, time and time again. Now, with something so ugly laid before her, she could no longer refute it.

God was mocking her poor judgment.

"You took the photos because you thought no one would believe you. You needed proof." A desensitized sort of understanding glazed Kenna's tone.

Jasmine produced a meager nod.

"What happened, exactly?"

"It was pouring rain. He ran Tyler off the road. I mean, I wasn't in the car, but I'd bet anything that's how it went down."

A chill wreathed her spine as she made a critical connection. The rain, the wreck. This was *the* car accident, the one that had scarred Dayton.

He'd escaped with minor cosmetic imperfections, with his life, while Tyler had been met with a cruel, irreversible fate.

Anger welled within her, but it was withheld information, rather than the young man's death, that served as the catalyst. Why hadn't he given her a detailed account of the accident? Could it have been that he still didn't trust her after all this time?

"His family and I advocated for charges to be brought against Dayton but there was some kind of medical complication standing in the way. So he just … got away with it."

Her anger morphed into choler of the highest degree. It sickened her that, somehow, he was able to use his illness as a loophole to evade the justice system.

"I didn't stop. I wanted to see that something was done. That it was properly investigated, at the very least." Jasmine tucked a lock of hair behind her ear. "He wasn't happy with my frequent visits to the police station. One day, he took me aside and told me that if I didn't drop my obsession over Tyler's death, he'd leak a video of me. He said he knew how to edit himself out, disguise his voice or whatever, and that he'd make sure everyone saw it. So I backed off."

Kenna lowered her voice, worried that Dayton was lingering somewhere outside the tent. "I've seen the tape. I could get it to you, and you could do whatever you want with it. Post it. Destroy it."

"You would do that?"

Would she? She was more or less on Dayton's team at this point. His ally. His accomplice, even. Would handing over the tape to Jasmine burn him completely?

If word got around that it was him in the video, he'd probably have his license revoked. His career as a psychiatrist would be over. Unless he started working under an assumed name. She didn't think jail time would factor into such a leak and that seemed to ease the decision for her.

"I would," she assured.

"Are you still going through with this?"

No matter how horrible the death of her boyfriend must have been, Jasmine was oblivious to the scope of Kenna's situation. The coercion-laced engagement and the marriage that was more of an insurance policy than a union of two souls. And yet, love was part of the equation; a dark, twisted bastardization of its original form, but it was love nonetheless.

"We're already married on paper. Today is just for show."

Dayton

Jasmine swept out of the tent, unfolding her sunglasses and replacing them on her face as she started walking in the direction of the trail that led back to the main road.

Rage boiled within him. Had he lost all control, he would have followed her, demanding to know why she'd had the nerve to show her face on his wedding day.

Dayton stood with his back to the wall of the tent. He bottled his breath, afraid the slightest movement or sound would give him away. Kenna soon emerged and he grabbed her roughly by the wrist, dragging her into the trees, away from the reception space, away from the site of the ceremony.

He couldn't risk anyone being within earshot.

"You knew she was coming, didn't you? That's why you made me sign the marriage license ahead of time."

"You signed it of your own volition, mind you, to get on my insurance plan. Don't pretend any differently."

"You *knew*."

"Kenna, I haven't spoken to her in years, not since—"

"Since what? Since you murdered her boyfriend?"

His hand pressed firmly over her mouth.

"You'd do well not to shout." Her eyes widened with shock and she nodded beneath his hand. She was his fretful lamb, pulse jumping at the prospect of slaughter. He inhaled deeply, attempting to steady himself. "Listen to me. I didn't kill that boy. What happened was a horrible accident."

Trusting she wouldn't scream, he removed his hand.

"And Lacey?" she volleyed with venom. "I suppose that was another horrible accident?"

"Come now, darling. It is our wedding day, after all. We can save our quarrels for a rainy day." He yanked her by the arm and they set out at a snail's pace in the direction of the ceremony. "We're going to go back out there and finish our vows. You'll cry on cue, and kiss me upon the priest's order. You're going to smile as we enter the reception as husband and wife, and you'll lay your head on my shoulder as we take our first dance. What you will not do is give anyone any indication that something is wrong. Am I clear?"

"Crystal."

When they returned to the altar, they were the epitome of a happy couple. No one in attendance could have known anything was amiss; with the exception of Carmen, who shot him an arched brow from her seat in the front row.

They exchanged vows. Not a single tear was shed. Kenna played along with it all. His compliant little actress. Even her kiss felt genuine.

He wasn't fooled.

Beneath that plastered-on behavior, he knew she was furious. Hurt. Terrified. An amalgam of all three.

She took his hand and allowed him to lead her onto the dance floor as the opening notes of *Are You Lonesome Tonight* sounded over the loudspeaker. How appropriate it was, that a breakup song was their first dance. She clasped her hands around his neck and laid her head on his chest. And, though she was merely following the terse instructions he'd given her in the woods, happiness blossomed beneath the spot where her cheek rested.

But when the song ended and they broke apart, whatever precious warmth and affection she'd spared had vanished. Her green eyes pierced him, sharp and unforgiving. It was a look that communicated a thousand things without saying anything at all.

And it was the last she gave him as she slunk away to mingle with the guests.

1 3

DEPARTURES

Kenna

One perk of being married: she'd been granted access to Dayton's finances. Once she was free to leave the reception, she had made full use of the resource and bought a plane ticket to Syracuse Hancock.

One-way.

It wasn't that Kenna intended to hide away in New York forever but she certainly couldn't imagine stomaching a return anytime soon. Not with the state of things.

"Runaway bride?" the older TSA agent joked as she passed through the screening machine.

On instinct, she glanced down at the wedding gown that she still wore. She had gone home to hastily pack a bag, but it hadn't occurred to her to change. Part of her thought the gown was too beautiful to wear anything else for her first-ever flight. A larger part wanted to show up on the farm exactly as she'd appeared at the altar. Let her sisters in on the magical wedding of which she was robbed.

She smiled weakly. Her heart hurt far too much to entertain humor. "Not exactly."

"Well, congratulations, young lady. I hope you find whatever it is you're looking for."

Grabbing her bag from the automated belt, she headed off to find her gate. As someone who'd never set foot in an airport, she found it hard to navigate. It was also overwhelming, and her distress and fatigue only intensified everything. The terminal was loud, buzzing with conversations and announcements that seemed to come through the intercom in an endless stream. Bright lights shone overhead and she was met with digital display boards overloaded with information at every turn. Finally, Kenna broke down and asked someone if they could point her in the right direction.

A lady stood behind a counter, attention glued to a computer, and above her head a screen proclaimed that boarding wouldn't begin for another hour.

She chose a seat away from everyone else, yearning to be alone with her thoughts. Jasmine had shown up and confirmed the thing she'd only fleetingly entertained.

Dayton was a killer.

Her heart knocked against her chest plate and she grew hot, itchy within the layers of silk which held her prisoner.

Suddenly, she wished she had changed into something more comfortable. Looser. She was trapped in her mind, her dress. But, in an hour's time, she'd no longer be trapped in Oregon.

Dayton

While the day had gotten off to a surreal start with Kenna's romantic confession, whatever magic had danced through the air turned to dust as the golden sun hung behind the trees. It was a picture-perfect ending to what had largely been a lovely day.

Lovely, if Dayton pretended that his bride hadn't been ripped from the ceremony by one of his many ex-lovers. Lovely, if he pretended that, though they had shared a dance not long ago, Kenna was nowhere to be found.

He racked his brain. She'd made no mention of leaving and yet her fiery hair was missing from the sea of people gathered in the tent.

Dayton spotted Nathan across the room and crossed the dance floor in haste. His friend balanced two cups in one hand as he refilled them, and they wobbled slightly, as if he'd been startled by Dayton's sudden appearance.

"Have you seen Kenna?" he asked.

"Not since your first dance." Nathan wrinkled his nose. The small action raised his glasses enough to obscure his eyebrows. "You think she took off? Maybe that woman she was talking to earlier had something to do with it. She looked kind of familiar, was she—"

"Not now, Nate. My wife is missing from our *wedding*."

Nathan latched a hand onto his shoulder and squeezed. "I said it once and I'll say it again. Karma's doing a number on you today, my friend." Releasing him, he sobered, adding, "Look, try not to worry too much. She might've gone home."

Searching his friend's eyes, Dayton suppressed a breath to keep his fury at bay. "You're right. I'm sure that's it."

Once Nathan wandered off toward the table where Charlaine waited, Dayton yanked his phone out of his pants pocket and dialed Kenna's number. The low purr of the dial tone competing with the upbeat music filtering through the sound system created a maddening effect that had him jabbing the 'end call' icon on the phone before its final ring.

He had no doubt that Jasmine had inspired Kenna's unannounced exit. Rooted to the linoleum, Dayton wondered if any action on his part would've resulted in a different outcome. Perhaps, if he'd taken the initiative to sit her down and explain his side of things, she wouldn't have been as shell-shocked.

It was, of course, no use to muse over it. No amount of theorizing had the power to transport her back to the reception.

Something cracked in front of his face and shattered his reverie.

"Hey you," Carmen said, snapping her fingers. "Is your heart about to go berserk? You've got a funny look on your face."

He retrieved his keys and slapped them into her palm. "I need a favor. Drive to the house and see if Kenna's there."

Her dark eyes narrowed while one corner of her mouth twitched in a suggestion of a smile. "Done. And I might not bother you with an explanation today but you better believe, come tomorrow, I'll want one, brother."

Each minute Carmen was away was more punishing than the last. Dayton was astonished by his ability to mingle and speak to guests as he waited for word from his sister. A series of images had hijacked his mind.

Kenna, lying on the floor, foaming at the mouth.

Her mangled body, dead in a ditch.

Red rivulets streaming down the side of his tub, razor blade in a bloody puddle.

A short, frustrated breath left his lips and he muttered a prayer to himself, as if keeping an open line of communication with God were key to surviving the abrupt uncertainty of a day that was practically guaranteed to go right.

Upon reciting the prayer several times through, Dayton felt a minor calm wash over him. It was, he realized, highly unlikely that Kenna had been involved in an accident or chosen to end her life as a result of her exchange with Jasmine. Logically, he understood this, but his brain had a predisposition for drumming up the darkest scenarios.

His ringtone sounded within his pocket. Seconds later, he stepped out of the tent and into the gray evening, putting the receiver to his ear as an ominous thunderclap rocked the sky.

"Well?"

"The bedroom's a mess. Drawers half open. Clothes on the floor, the bed. I'm guessing she packed a bag. Do you have any idea where she might have gone? A friend she might stay with?"

"No, I don't know, Carmen, because *if* I knew, I'd be at her friend's house instead of hanging around my own reception, alone."

"Look, I completely understand that you're upset, but you don't have to be a dick. I came over here to help you look for Kenna."

"I'm sorry." Running his tongue along his teeth, he tried once more, "And you're absolutely sure she's not there?"

"Like I said, she's gone."

Rain sprinkled Dayton's screen as he terminated the call. Thunder cracked overhead. Lightning flashed.

A deer stood off in the distance, statuesque. They seemed to hold each other's gaze for a moment, but another clap of thunder kicked it into motion and it ran away, zigzagging through the trees.

14

THE O'CALLAGHANS

Kenna

She asked the taxi driver to let her out at the mailbox. From there, it was a two-mile trek. Kenna needed every minute that walk afforded to gather her thoughts and, even then, she wondered if any amount of time would've been enough for a moment like this. Reuniting with the family she'd left behind for a better life. While it hadn't always been the best, it was a life all her own.

That was all she'd ever wanted.

Looking to her right, she took in the orchard's symmetrical rows of trees and their many branches feathered with brilliant green. She couldn't see the pink flowers from this distance, but she knew they were there, slowly budding beneath the summer sun. Her chest tightened as she surveyed the familiar sight, brain flooded with memories flashing like a pull-chain light, flickering and then gone.

The sunburns. The complaints. Chasing her sisters through the maze of trees. The starry nights and dewy mornings when that plot of land was alive with the O'Callaghan girls' screams and laughter.

Nostalgia gave way to nerves as Kenna neared the house. The tin-roofed structure seemed much too small to accommodate a family of eight, but growing up it never felt crowded, even with all of the girls sharing a bedroom. A chicken coop, in a terrible state of disrepair, was off to the side of the house. Little noise came from the hens within.

Her hand froze on the porch railing as something piqued her interest. A pair of bicycles lay in the grass.

Though they were a normal part of childhood for many, her parents had expressly forbidden any of the girls from riding—let alone owning—one.

Had things become more relaxed since she'd left?

Heart thundering, Kenna swung the squeaky screen door open and knocked. Five long years had passed since she'd seen any of her family and she worried she wouldn't be able to tell some of the girls apart. Some of that doubt subsided when the main door crept inward and she was faced with Fallon, the oldest of her younger sisters.

Her red hair was longer and there was a tired quality to her eyes, but other than that, she looked much the same.

Fallon didn't launch into hysterics.

She assessed Kenna, a fine line creasing between her brows. "Thought the next time I'd be seein' you would be in a wooden box, not a dress."

Kenna stood there. Not blinking, not speaking.

"Why've you come here now? Wearing such a thing?"

"I didn't have anywhere else to go."

Fallon's eyes fell to the bruises on her wrists, which Kenna immediately concealed, but she knew the damage was done.

"Well, you better come inside, then."

The stained and torn couch had been replaced. Other than that, the house hadn't changed. Cream wallpaper, discolored by her father's cigarette smoke. Family photos in which they'd been asked not to smile. Shelves cluttered with Bibles, cookbooks, and an old set of encyclopedias, which her father wanted to get rid of but their mother had argued were a good supplement for their home-schooling. There were no games, which her parents were convinced would either encourage the girls' imaginations or lead them down the path of the degenerate gambler. Worst of all, it'd result in both.

Kenna and Fallon settled in at the dinner table, somewhere they had convened countless times. But this meeting felt like their first one.

"Where'd you run off to all these years? You never would tell us when you'd call."

"Oregon."

"Say, isn't that where that girl turned up dead? They're looking for the killer."

Unbelievable. Even her sheltered sisters on the other side of the country knew about the Lacey Greene homicide.

"Did you guys get a television?"

"Mama hasn't gone that soft. But she gives us free range of the radio. I like listening to the news, in a way. Hearing about all the horrible things out there makes me feel blessed that God chose to protect us with these walls."

The implication that their mother was in charge gave her pause but it all came together as her gaze swept the room.

A shrill pinging filled her ears as she stared at the green and white paisley urn sitting on a shelf. A picture of her father rested beside it. Pain lashed at her insides.

For all the times he'd struck her, saddled her with extra chores, told her going to college wasn't part of God's plan, she actually felt something when faced with the reality of his death. And maybe it wasn't the loss that stirred something within her, but the not knowing.

"Papa," she started, waiting a moment for the quaver to abandon her voice. "He's gone?"

"The smoking finally did him in. For someone who preached about the evil of indulgence so much, he sure didn't bother quittin'." The faintest hint of brogue came out as she added softly, "Tried calling. You never picked up."

She thought back to last fall. All of the calls she'd ignored. Guilt snaked through her. She should've realized something was wrong.

Kenna placed her hand over her sister's.

"Fallon, I'm sorry I wasn't here to help with the funeral or with the girls or with anything else the last five years. Honestly, when I left, I didn't take into consideration that everything would be on you."

"After you left, we were all jealous. Mama and Papa went to bed and we'd sit around a kerosene lamp on the bedroom floor and take turns sayin' where we'd go. The fun wore off after a little while. Some of us wondered if you were dead. But then you called that first Christmas." Fallon laid a hand over her heart. "That was the best present we ever got."

Kenna was exhausted from traveling and didn't possess the energy required for such a conversation, but her attempt to steer their talk in a different direction was thwarted with another truth that was hard to swallow.

"How did you like Jamesville?"

"Since you left us for college, they decided we didn't need to go to public school. They said it put too many ideas in your head, corrupted you. Really, I think they didn't want to lose any more of us."

It was hard enough to say sorry and mean it the first time. She wouldn't do it again. She tried another question.

"Where is everyone? It's so quiet."

"In the schoolhouse, out back. Jeremiah helped Papa build it before … you know. Taryn's leading lessons. She does her homework after sundown."

"Jeremiah?"

"My husband."

Coming home was quickly shaping up to be more than Kenna could handle. Had she made a mistake? Should she have hid out somewhere in Oregon?

No, Dayton would've made quick work of tracking her down and dragging her home.

"You're married?" It wasn't entirely ludicrous. Fallon was 19. All the same, it came as a shock.

"You do what you have to do to keep things running." Fallon nodded at her dress. "From the looks of it, you've just tied the knot yourself. Not so nice of a gentleman, judging by those marks."

"It's complicated."

"Yeah? Everything is, I reckon. Me? I didn't marry Jeremiah because I loved him. Papa died and we needed someone around to help run things. And, with Mama so out of it, I didn't see another choice." Seeing the look on her sister's face, Fallon pointed a finger. "Don't you pity me. It's not like I hate the man."

An uncomfortable laugh of understanding, and perhaps commiseration, bubbled up from Kenna's lungs and Fallon produced a subdued one of her own. They sat in each other's company, quietly smiling.

A band of voices sounded outside, followed by the squeaking and clicking of both doors. Once the girls were inside, the joyous noise stopped. They all displayed some degree of awe upon seeing their long-lost sister seated at the table. The shock passed quickly and a unique reaction manifested within each of them. Taryn swept off to the bedroom, no words or expression to give anything away.

Rory and Delaney barreled toward her and nearly knocked her out of the chair, swarming her with hugs and shrieking 'Kenna,' over and over, in delight.

And yet Kenna's tears didn't surface until she spotted a girl who had big, green eyes and frizzy braids and wore a dress that was two inches too long. A pang shot through her. Oona, who had been a baby when she'd left, was now a slight 6-year-old.

Rather than run to Kenna as her older sisters had done, Oona slowly approached Fallon, asking, "Who's that lady?"

Fallon wrapped an arm around her shoulders, turning Oona to face Kenna, and spoke calmly. "You remember sometimes we'd talk about McKenna?"

She nodded her little head and tears streamed down Kenna's cheeks. It was hard to listen to her sister's attempt to excavate the memory of her, as if she hadn't once existed alongside the rest of them.

"You left," Oona said, with all the blunt directness one expected of a child.

"I did."

"Are you staying?"

"For a while."

Oona gave her a final, uncertain look before running outside to play with Rory and Delaney.

"Care to help with dinner? Once you change."

In the cramped bathroom, Kenna fought and forged her way out of the wedding dress. She banged her knees and elbows on the cabinets and the tub as she shimmied around. She had to break the zipper in order to free herself. Once she stood in her underwear, gown pooled on the floor, she winced, rubbing all the spots that were sure to sport bruises the following morning.

Her phone stared back at her within her open suitcase. Cold sweat beaded on her forehead. Squatting, she tapped the screen to life. No signal. Which meant no messages. No calls.

The sweat dissipated. Her muscles relaxed.

She threw on a t-shirt and sweatpants and joined Fallon in the kitchen. Kenna fell into the rhythmic tasks as if she'd never left. Rinsing, peeling, and dicing. While she could prep ingredients for hours, the actual cooking was better left to someone else. Her sister wasted no time teasing her in that regard.

"Didn't they teach you how to become the world's greatest chef at that college of yours?"

"I'm the reason God invented countertop appliances and you know it." Kenna smiled faintly to herself. "They do have culinary schools, but they're miles different from my university."

Fallon set a glass dish in the oven, then straightened to her full height and frowned. "Have you not graduated?"

"Technically, yes, I graduated from one program. But now I'm in graduate school. I have one more year, plus certifications, licensing …" she trailed off. Things had been so grim lately, she'd forgotten that the incredible milestone of obtaining her master's degree loomed on the not-so-distant horizon.

"What kind of work will that prepare you for?"

"Mental health counseling. Essentially, I'll sit in a room with someone, listen to them, and help them find solutions to their problems." It was a tremendous oversimplification of what the job entailed, but Kenna thought it was the best way to present it to someone outside of the psychology realm. "Dayton, my husband, does similar work. He's a doctor. A psychiatrist."

"A doctor. My, my." Fallon fanned herself. Nodding to Kenna's wrists, she added, "Good thing because you'll need a doctor to see to those bruises."

"We had a disagreement. I turned to leave and he grabbed me too hard. It was an accident, really. It's not like it's happened before." As Kenna spoke the words, she registered their falsity. What ran through her head was too dark to divulge to her sister.

Those small, occasional marks Dayton left on her body—bite marks, scrapes, bruises—were concrete evidence of their love. A love that she was so unsure of yet desperately needed. She often likened it to a straight-laced kid toying with the idea of drugs; she could be clearheaded or she could choose something that would make her feel otherworldly and, if given the choice, who could deny themselves that?

That transcendental feeling was worth far more than the defects he brandished her with.

Her sister's voice brought her back to the present. "I just want to see you taken care of properly, is all. I may not love Jeremiah, but he's a good man, with a good heart. He'd never hurt me. Never hurt any of us, for that matter."

When it came time for the meal, her mother finally made an appearance. She emerged from her bedroom in one of the same, tired gowns she'd always worn. Her face looked just as ragged. It seemed she'd aged too quickly over the years Kenna had spent away from home; whether it was due to her husband's death or her eldest daughter's absence, she did not know.

The fiery red had faded from her hair, leaving it a muted orange. Her eyes now possessed a glassy quality that—paired with the tattered dress—gave her a haunting appearance.

Moira O'Callaghan's hand flew to her chest and she took a few stumbling steps backward like she'd seen an apparition. Kenna stood perfectly still and remained silent, not wanting to overload her mother's senses. She approached her daughter slowly, cautiously, expression shifting with every step. Kenna had many years to prepare herself for this reunion, which was why she did not flinch when her mother raised a hand to strike her across the face.

The sharp sting spread from her cheek to her temple. Rather than crying out or cradling her face, Kenna steeled her features and stared down her mother, eyes aflame with inextinguishable determination.

"Your father is dead." She made it sound like a punishment. Like it was her fault. "You left us, for what? Some silly school? That was more important to you than your family."

"I couldn't breathe here, Mama. You and Papa didn't support the vision I had for my life. To get an education, to see some stretch of this country outside of the orchard."

"And what about the Lord's vision, McKenna? Do you think

He'd approve of you putting your selfish desires above the needs of your own flesh and blood? I hope you've been repenting long and often all these years."

"I've missed you all terribly, but I won't apologize for leaving."

Her mother studied her for what felt like an eternity, searching for something she'd never find.

Having Dayton in her life had restructured her. The pieces of Kenna her mother had once known were a memory so distant, it was as if they'd never been a part of her.

At last, she said, "I'll tell everyone dinner is ready."

The O'Callaghan girls, resembling a small army, soon filed into the main area of the home. Jeremiah sat in what was formerly her father's chair. He was a short man with dark blonde hair. His rolled shirt sleeves revealed muscled, tan forearms that were a result of laboring under the summer sun. He nodded politely as Fallon introduced them.

Delaney said grace. The majority of the meal carried on in silence. No one was quite sure what to say and so they said nothing at all.

Sitting there, among her sisters and mother, Kenna had never felt more like a stranger. It was terrible to feel so out of place in a home that was so familiar. Her fork froze midway to her plate as she was hit with a disquieting thought.

Dayton had become her family.

Not long after dinner, all of the girls crammed together in their bedroom. A kerosene lamp burned bright in the middle of the floor. Shadows danced on the walls and ceiling. There were six identical white wrought iron twin beds, three on either side of the room, lined up in an orphanage-like fashion.

Kenna found it odd that her parents had kept her bed. They weren't ones to hold onto things that no longer served a purpose. Had they kept it in the hope that, one day, she might return? An ache spread through her chest. She'd told her mother she hadn't regretted leaving and, though that was true, she couldn't help but feel like she'd been a horrible daughter, and an even worse sister.

The separation from her parents had never been difficult for Kenna, but being apart from her sisters was like walking around with a burn wound on her heart that refused to heal, skewering her with raw, tender, pulsing hurt.

Swallowing, she was grateful the relative darkness of the room hid the tears misting in her eyes.

Once they were sure the younger girls had fallen asleep, Fallon, Taryn, and Kenna deemed it safe to talk amongst themselves. Taryn, who was on the cusp of 16, remained staunchly opposed to interacting with her estranged sister, refusing to even make eye contact. She sat alongside them, nonetheless, alert and listening.

"Where does Jeremiah sleep?"

"Oh, he and I usually sleep in the schoolhouse, but I told him I'll be sleeping in here for as long as you're staying." Fallon mumbled, "Not that he's bothered by it." She licked her lips and Kenna could tell she was wrestling with something she'd rather not say. "McKenna, why've you come home? Are you in trouble of some kind?"

"I needed to clear my head."

Fallon eyed her doubtfully. "On your wedding day?"

Telling her sister the full story was unwise, but she'd offer them a small truth. "That girl who went missing … the one who was murdered? Well, my husband and I have a connection to her."

At this, Taryn's head snapped in her direction. "You're kidding."

"What kind of connection?" Fallon pressed, eager to have something other than the bruises to further condemn Dayton. There was no denying they were related.

"She was almost his patient. She came in one day, panicking, and sat in his office long enough for him to figure out that her boyfriend didn't treat her the best. Then she bolted. Months later, she was found dead."

"How can people be so cruel? Going around and killing each other? And you went out there willingly, beyond our fence." Fallon shook her head.

Timidly, Taryn spoke up. "I'd like to go out there someday."

Fallon shot her younger sister a look of disbelief, throwing a hand in the air. "And wind up in a garbage heap?"

"What time I am afraid, I will trust in thee."

"Don't quote Psalms at me, missy." Fallon grabbed Kenna's wrist, forcing Taryn to acknowledge it. "Take a good, hard look. You leave this home and this is what awaits you. McKenna is evidence enough happiness won't be there to greet you with open arms."

Jerking back her arm, Kenna met her sister's gaze. "You know as well as I do that Taryn is under no obligation to stay here once she comes of age. She'll be free to do whatever she'd like."

"And what of me? Why was I not granted the same?"

"Convince Mama to sell the land. Move into town and immerse yourselves in the real world. Sure, there are bad people every-where you go, but most of them are good, Fallon, and it won't serve you to doubt or fear everyone you come across."

Fallon rose. With a quaver of irritation in her voice, she announced, "I'm going to check on Jeremiah."

Taryn was unfazed by her sister barging out of the room. "So, what's college like?"

Kenna regaled her with tales from her time at Ponderosa and Taryn had what felt like a dozen follow-up questions with the conclusion of each one. She patiently answered all of her sister's queries, relishing this time together while simultaneously wondering when she'd see her next.

Coming home had never crossed Kenna's mind as she toiled away at university but, in the span of one day, she absorbed the magnitude of everything she'd missed out on in her sisters' lives. She hadn't even been there for them when their father died, and while that loss didn't affect her much, the fact that she had failed to support her grieving sisters did not sit well with her.

"I could help you apply, you know. To colleges. If that's what you really want, then you shouldn't let anything stand in the way. You deserve to get out of here and get a real education." Kenna glanced at her ring then back at her sister. "Fall in love."

"And if I end up married to a crazy doctor?"

"You won't." Kenna smiled weakly as she leaned over the foot of her bed and blew out the kerosene lamp. In the dark, she whispered, "You're too good for that."

15

DYING ANIMAL

Kenna

A firm rapping at the door interrupted Kenna's pleasant morning. She had slept soundly, and now she was dressed in her former, conservative garb, eating a bowl of oatmeal and going about some semblance of morning routine as if she'd never left her family.

The knock was a breach of the familiar.

Taryn headed for the front door, spying through the curtain. "There's a man outside."

"Mr. Johnson here to pick up his eggs?" Fallon inquired from the kitchen. She was up to her elbows in mess. Flour dusted every surface, herself included. Tacky dough covered her palms and fingers as she halted mid-knead.

"It isn't Mr. Johnson."

"Out with it, then. Who is it?"

"Dunno. I'm not opening it."

"Why ever not?" Fallon shot Taryn a look that said *so I have to do everything around here* before scrubbing her hands in the sink and migrating to the door.

Standing in the way of her sister, a startling intensity etched itself into Taryn's features. "Don't let him in here. He's got the devil in his eyes."

Her gut churned at the comment and Kenna became fearful of her own mind as it conjured an image of what might have been on the other side of that door. Staccato breathing filled her ears as she pictured a foreboding man with a scarred face and dark hair, standing against a blackened sky.

It was pure madness even entertaining the idea that Dayton was the one idling on the porch, and yet something in the way her insides knotted refuted it was anyone else.

If it was him, how had he *found* her?

Ignoring her younger sister's plea, Fallon opened the door and her face went slack. There was a low hum of a male's voice and then she nodded, stepping aside. Heavy footfalls grabbed the attention of everyone inside.

Kenna's grip tightened on her spoon.

The devil in his eyes. Kenna knew precisely what her sister had meant. She had seen it that fateful night at St. James, and yet she had pressed on in her involvement with him.

Over the last 48 hours, she had cycled through the same questions, again and again, becoming less sure of her answers with each repetition.

Why had she been so insistent about the mentorship when she had a bad feeling about him from the start? Why had she entertained even the *idea* of a romantic relationship? Why hadn't she told Reynolds that day in the diner that, yes, Dayton was more than likely responsible for Lacey Greene's death. She had not done this because she had nothing to tell. Reynolds wouldn't have cuffed Dayton based on her speculation.

From her limited understanding of the law, there must not

have been enough evidence—or perhaps any at all—linking him to the murder.

Hence why he now stood in her family's farmhouse.

Dayton wore his standard non-work attire, besides the athleisure he was fond of. Dark jeans and a flannel. For all the fury she gleaned in his eyes, he didn't shout. He stood tall, shoulders and jaw squared. He didn't acknowledge her sisters. His tense words were meant for her alone.

"There's a cab waiting on the main road."

"No."

"No?" Dayton cocked his head, tone on par with a parent challenging a disobedient child.

"No, I'm not going with you."

A look of minor irritation crossed his face. Kenna had witnessed it on many occasions, usually after he'd received a call from a healthcare provider about an insurance claim she'd botched for one of his patients.

The screen door squeaked as he grabbed something off the porch while one foot remained inside. He dropped a duffel bag on the ground, mercilessly holding her gaze as he did so. "I thought you might say that."

Dayton

The O'Callaghan farmhouse felt much smaller than how it looked from the outside. It bordered on claustrophobic. The ceiling extended only a few inches above his head. Between that and the many sets of eyes on him, on top of the traveler's fatigue, he felt ill. There was no time for weakness or vomiting spells. He'd come to bring Kenna home.

He only prayed her reluctance could be overcome.

Five girls with Kenna's blazing red hair sat around the table, a glass of orange juice and plate of breakfast in various stages of consumption before them all. It was a strange way to encounter her siblings for the first time.

These unmoving, uneating girls who all looked troublingly similar to one another, like a set of nesting dolls.

The smallest girl abandoned her chair and approached him. She extended a hand. "How'd you do? I'm Oona."

A great deal of time had passed since his last experience with children. His first year of residency, he'd been assigned to a youth wing of a psychiatric ward. And, while he occasionally encountered kids at the emergency room, the patients he was assigned were almost exclusively adults.

Dayton kneeled on one knee and gently shook her hand, offering a warm smile. "Very nice to meet you. And what a beautiful name you have."

"I used to think it was funny." She toyed with the end of her braid. "We have breakfast."

He almost laughed at the youthful directness of her words, that roundabout invitation. Instead, he let Oona guide him to an empty chair and sat down among his gaggle of sisters-in-law. The tension that laced his entrance was seemingly forgotten.

"Everyone," Kenna began, clearly unhappy that she had to offer an introduction. "This is my husband, Dayton."

Other than a few polite hellos, no one made any attempt at conversation. The girls carried on with breakfast and their curious green eyes drifted to him every so often.

Once the meal had ended, he wasted no time executing his plan. He stepped halfway out onto the porch and directed a comment to Kenna, hoping that his icy tone was enough to earn her compliance. "I'd like to speak with you. Alone."

Kenna followed him out the door and they wandered away from the house and into the orchard. They walked and walked for what must have been half an hour and the sheer amount of land laid out before them was never-ending.

The sun shone, bright and brilliant, but its heat was far from oppressive. Dayton pushed up his sleeves and blew overlong strands of hair out of his face. Beside him, Kenna was near unrecognizable.

She wore a thin, loose, long-sleeve top tucked into a skirt that revealed no trace of skin. The same way her siblings dressed, in these overly modest, homemade garments. Her usual boots were replaced by white canvas sneakers.

Even while clad in the glorified sheet, she was the most beautiful thing he'd ever seen. Just as beautiful as she'd been on their wedding day.

He ventured a question—whose answer he already knew—if only to hear her speak.

Her silence was his own personal hell.

"Is this what your parents make all of you wear?"

"Did you honestly bring us all the way out here to ask me that?" Her lips formed a thin line, as if she regretted her words. "My father's dead."

"I know." He drew in a breath that doubled as a moment of contemplation as Kenna arched a brow, growing increasingly expectant. Deceiving her had gotten him nowhere. "I've known since last year."

Her voice was calm. "You knew all this time?"

No apology formed on his lips. Dayton looked at her like one might look at a dying animal, the understanding that the living, breathing thing before him would soon be broken beyond repair.

"All this time, and you didn't say anything? My own *father*. You kept it from me. You bastard." Kenna raised her fists but he gently caught them before they made contact and she collapsed against him, shouting through sobs.

He stroked her back as she fell apart. The comforting gesture was all he found himself capable of.

Since his earlier attempt at speaking to Kenna had been thwarted by the revelation of her father's death—and her subsequent breakdown—he sequestered her again once everyone had gone to bed.

Worried they may have been overheard on the porch, she led him out to the small barn located behind the house. She told him it once housed pigs and goats, but they'd sold off the animals in the interim between their father's death and Fallon's marriage.

In the darkness, she scaled a ladder to the barren hayloft and, once she'd made it to the top, motioned for him to do the same. Kenna meandered into a corner. A series of locks clicked and he watched her pull and secure the twin hatches as the inky glow of the night sky flooded the space. Dayton sank against a wooden support beam and she nestled beside him as if they were two ordinary people on an ordinary night. He savored her proximity, however incongruous it was with the state of things.

"I used to come up here a lot," she said, as her hand sought his own. Had she forgotten the events of that afternoon? He surmised she was experiencing some kind of shock and, as a result, it subdued whatever her true reaction might have been. "I'd look at the stars and the moon, fantasize about leaving and never coming back. The fact that I succeeded … well, I suppose I'm back now. But coming up here, those dreams I had, it all seems like another lifetime ago. It's bizarre."

Kenna was so well adjusted that he found it hard to believe she'd grown up this way, sharing a bedroom the size of his living room with five other girls. Living off the grid with very limited access to technology, of which she was now a master. Of course, she had attended public high school. That explained her proficiency with computers and the like.

But her story never quite made sense.

How had she gotten a Greyhound ticket? How had she known where to go once she arrived in Branch Spring? Where had she gone? And how had she applied and gotten into Ponderosa under the watchful eye of her strict parents?

Let alone on a scholarship.

His thumb performed lazy strokes on her shoulder. "There's something I've always wanted to ask you. Something I haven't been able to figure out."

"Oh?" She squeezed genuine surprise out of the single syllable.

"How is it that you made it to Branch Spring? You got into Ponderosa on a scholarship. All of that is quite impressive for a teenage runaway who was raised as a shut-in. Dare I say it's unbelievable."

"I had a guidance counselor who was exceptionally kind. Without his help, I'd probably still be stuck here."

His. It was that hissing, possessive pronoun that ignited a quiet fire within him. Rather than torturing himself by imagining what she'd done in exchange for that help, Dayton kept a level head.

"Then I am grateful to him. My life would be incomplete without you, lamb. Despite what you think."

He toyed with the cuff of her modest dress, still in disbelief that she'd worn the generic garments for the first 18 years of her life. The plain clothing offered no chance for expression or exploration of self. Back in Oregon, Kenna frequently wore light-colored, gauzy blouses. They resembled a modern adaptation of the O'Callaghan family wardrobe. Dayton wondered if it was an unconscious nod to her upbringing.

"The way you grew up was regime-like. Your parents, the family they raised you in, it's no better than a cult. Know that I'm not saying this to offend you. It's my honest observation."

She scoffed. "As a psychiatrist, I'd expect you to know a little something about perspective."

"We're intimate, Kenna. I can't view you or your life through an impartial lens." After a moment's hesitation, he added, "Listen, if you're open to it, maybe we should consider having some of the girls move in with us. Even if it's on a temporary basis."

"Do you honestly think I'd want any of them near *you?*"

"They're your sisters," he bit back, a little too forcefully. "You can't leave them here to live like this."

"This is all they know."

A long silence engulfed them as they both stared out into the starless night. This was clearly a difficult topic for her and he wouldn't push further.

"Why are you here?"

"To bring you home." Dayton breathed the confession into the crown of her head and cradled her closer. She jerked away. Hands planted on the floor, she leaned back and fixed him with a hard look.

"Believe it or not, my aim in marrying you wasn't to become another number in your body count."

"And what exactly was your aim, darling?"

Her expression softened, if only a little. "I guess I thought I was capable of helping you through all of this."

"You are." Gently, he took her wrists but released them just as quick upon spying the fading bruises he'd left behind. "Do you remember the first night I invited you over?"

"The drugging. The choking. The threats. How could I forget, darling?" Her tone was mockingly vicious on the last word.

"That night, before you left, you told me something. Something that stuck with me. Haunted me. You said if you couldn't save me, no one could. And you didn't know it then, but that is the cold, hard truth. You are my light, my love, my guide, my last sliver of hope. Come *home*. We'll find a way to make this work."

"Translation: you'll find a way to keep me quiet and obedient? Tell me, is this relationship even real or is it just an elaborate con to make sure I don't speak out against you?"

"This relationship is whatever you'd like it to be," he said honestly. "For whatever duration."

"And if I want something I shouldn't?"

Dayton didn't want her answer. He needed it. It was essential to the continuing function of his being. Whatever she desired was as vital to him as oxygen. His throat burned as he coaxed the words out. "What do you want, lamb?"

"I want it to be real." Kenna delicately traced the scar along his cheek, her gaze flitting from his eyes to the rippled skin. "When you tell me you love me, I don't want to wonder if it's genuine or if you're being manipulative. No more games."

"No more games," he repeated, resting his forehead against hers.

Plenty of variables were left up in the air. The promise wasn't backed by one hundred percent of his confidence but he'd given it anyway, out of desperation.

Losing her would cost him everything.

16

FIGHT OR FLIGHT

Dayton

Saying goodbye to Kenna's family the following morning was a somber affair. There were no tears but everyone wore mournful expressions. Perhaps they wondered if this was truly the last time they'd ever see her.

Dayton wouldn't stand for that. Just as he wouldn't stand to watch these brilliant, capable girls waste away on this orchard when there was so much more waiting for them beyond those trees.

When it was his turn to hug Fallon, he whispered in her ear, "If any of you wish to spend a summer with us out west, it can be arranged. I've left our contact information beneath the French press."

She looked up at him, a quiet kindness in her eyes. "Thank you."

.   .   .

Kenna refused to speak to him during their onslaught of cab rides, layovers, and flights. She remained impossibly quiet as they headed home in the sports car.

Was she punishing him for ripping her away from her family? She had agreed to come home with him. Their night in the barn had been the definition of conciliatory and now she was giving him the cold shoulder.

He was tempted to put some Leonard Cohen on and pray that her annoyance translated to speech.

Amid the deafening quiet, his mind wandered.

He hadn't been able to keep up with the manhunt in Syracuse—no cell reception—but he conducted a quick search during one of their layovers while Kenna was in the restroom.

Still no sign of Sanders.

There was some speculation about the search dwindling down. They'd spent too much time, wasted too many resources. Some sites took it a step further with their criticism. It wasn't as if they were tracking down a serial killer. This was someone responsible for one murder and it was being sensationalized because it happened in small-town USA and the victim was a white sorority girl. That was the awful truth.

Dayton fought to focus on the road as a fresh wave of anxiety gripped him. He was frightened by a possibility that was dangerously close to becoming a reality.

What if Sanders was never located?

Reynolds, in his fervor to solve the case, would circle back to him—with or without the approval of his lieutenant. Maybe he'd scrounge up enough support for another warrant, challenge his previous standard of thorough and find the large crawl space below the floor that he'd miraculously missed the first time around.

"Stop here," Kenna said, interrupting his thoughts.

He pulled off into the parking lot for Highway 18 Diner, assuming it was where she'd wanted to stop. They were on the edge of town and there was nothing else for several miles. The restaurant was small and resembled an airstream trailer with an aluminum-like exterior and a busted neon sign.

In one fluid motion, she unclicked her seatbelt and opened the door, glancing at him as she got out of the car. "Come on, Dr. Merino."

The slamming door punctuated her gentle demand.

His chest compressed. Is that what she'd decided during all of those non-speaking hours? That she'd revert to their old formalities. Distance herself. Pretend they weren't husband and wife.

He could handle her resistance, but he couldn't take her running off again.

Dayton held the diner door open for her and she mumbled a quiet word of thanks as he trailed her inside. Why she was so insistent on stopping there, he had no clue, but food certainly seemed like a good idea after their day of travel. Neither of them had eaten anything more substantial than a protein bar since the day prior.

Once they were settled in a grimy booth, Kenna folded her hands atop the table as if she were preparing to cross-examine him. "I want you to tell me what happened with Jasmine and Tyler. Your side of the story."

"Here?"

She blew out a concentrated breath.

"We're in a public place. I can't run away—it'd raise too much suspicion. There's no place better."

He darkened his gaze, prepared to reason with her. "Can't this wait until we've had a full night's rest?"

"No." She laughed. It was a short, soft sound. Deranged, almost. "No, I won't be able to sleep until I have something to counteract Jasmine's story. I need the missing pieces. So, talk. No more games, remember?"

17

TYLER

Dayton

ayton realized there was no way out of this. He'd have to tell her everything. He pulled in a series of calm, steady breaths and memorized every detail of Kenna's face, in case it was the last time he had the privilege to view it.

This was it. Their point of no return.

If she ever learned of Lacey, it would only drag her deeper into the muck.

Two stacks of huckleberry pancakes sat before them, and though they'd subsisted on lackluster airport fare the entire day, it seemed neither was hungry. It was their curse. Food went untouched wherever they went.

"Jasmine and I were involved for a semester."

"Of this, I'm aware." Kenna smiled but it was far from kind. "She was a patient of yours, obviously. What was she being seen for?"

"You know I can't tell you." Realization dawned on him like a cool breeze in the dead of summer. Unexpected but delightful.

"She didn't tell you? Oh, you must have found that highly frustrating. I've seen the notes on your computer. Very detailed."

She blanched. "You read my files?"

"What's yours is mine, or however the adage goes."

She recovered quickly. "If that's true, I suppose you'll lend me yours."

"What resides there would startle you far worse than these sob stories you run around collecting."

"Which is?"

He paused for a beat. "My true self."

Fascination and horror swirled in her eyes. Kenna lost the intrigue once she registered that the course of their conversation had veered.

"What was Jasmine being treated for? And don't give me any of that confidentiality nonsense. When it involves *these* girls, it's different."

"No, you're mistaken. It isn't any different. You see, you perceive a difference because you're one of them, and as a result of that you feel entitled to information that's still off-limits."

"You can't cherry-pick your ethics."

"No? I've made a career of it."

Even if it was a momentary lapse, he enjoyed seeing her riled. He'd conjured the reaction from her so easily during their mentorship. But she had hardened in her exposure to him, and so he took greater pride in her present slip.

She sipped her water between half-hearted nibbles of pancake and Dayton relished in her quiet contemplation, bursting out of his skin with anticipation.

What he didn't anticipate was an apology.

"Sorry. I know you can't hand over privileged information, no matter the perceived stakes. My ethics professor beat it into our heads every chance she got and even before then, you made sure I knew it." Pressing her lips together, Kenna slowly lifted her gaze to him. She spoke softly. "I'm on your side, alright? But that doesn't come free of expectations. As your partner, your lover, I deserve to hear whatever truth you're legally and ethically able to disclose."

Lover. The single syllable was a symphony to his ears, an adrenaline shot to his underpowered heart. The answer to his fiercest prayers.

"I'll grant you as much, if you're confident you can handle it."

She faltered. "As in?"

"It's high time we established some trust between us, don't you think? You told me 'no more games.' Well, I'd like to extend an expectation to you. No more silly little notes on your laptop. I expressly forbid you from breathing a word of this to anyone."

"Okay."

"During the time Jasmine was my patient, I learned she was in a relationship. I didn't put much stock in it, confident it'd be a nonissue when it came time for us to ..." he stopped himself. How strange it was to explain one of these encounters to her. His scalp prickled. Now *there* was a new observation. He made a mental note to add it to his research later that evening. "She slept with me without batting an eye, but she split her time between Tyler and me. That grated on me, her rushing out of my bed because she had to meet him somewhere. I felt the same way with you so much earlier on. When I found out about your date with Liam, I was furious. That's when I realized you weren't like the rest, that there was something special about you."

"And what might that be?" Skepticism clung to her every word.

"Your compassion. The understanding you so relentlessly seek. Your unending capacity to forgive."

Brows raised, Kenna picked at her plate. "Why didn't you say all of that at the altar?"

"I should have."

"How did you get her to consent to the tape?"

"Not by drugging her, if that's where your mind went. She was very enthusiastic, so long as it—"

"Stayed between the two of you."

"Right. I keep forgetting you've seen it."

"Only the first few minutes," she asserted, as if the distinction was of critical importance. "Your obsession with Tyler doesn't make sense. Not unless you—"

"I didn't love her." His tone was firmer than he'd intended. Voice, louder. A couple of patrons shot them wary glances.

"Explain it."

Kenna was performing a poor man's psychoanalysis on him. The restaurant was a sorry excuse for an office. There was no pleasant smell, no privacy. Grease and processed carbs filled the air. Sticky vinyl and dirty windows.

When Dayton checked the wall clock to see if his hour was up, it didn't matter what time it reflected. They weren't leaving until she got the answers she sought.

"There's a part of me that enjoys leaving the girls with nothing. And, maybe I find a strange solace in knowing that, even if it's only for a short while, they feel as empty as I do."

He sipped his decaf as she processed what had been said. He had been to death's door but it was never clearer than this moment, with Kenna in the diner, what his personal Hell was destined to look like. Answering, over and over again, for all the wrong he'd done. Explaining it to the one person he loved. The death and the drugs and the sex and the botched ethics and the overarching purpose for all of that madness of which she was clueless.

God willing, she'd remain that way.

"Charlee's boyfriend left her." She studied him with a muted delight that could only be described as wicked. A cat watching a goldfish circle its bowl before striking. "But you left her with something. A letter of rec."

"Don't view it as a favor or a good deed. I wanted her gone. It's less messy with fewer of you around." She flinched at his use of 'you' and he regretted it.

"If I'm just an 'n' in your population, just some piece of data to you." Kenna's arms performed short, jerky movements. He imagined her twisting her ring beneath the table. "Then why do you keep me around?"

"You're more than that. You're the outcome. I feel as if I've finally found someone I can trust. Completely. But we have to build that trust for the both of us. As I said earlier."

Tears clouded her eyes but her speech was sturdy as ever. Unswayed by emotion. She'd make a fine therapist one day.

"Tell me about the accident."

Kenna

Blinking rapidly, she rid her eyes of any trace of moisture. Now was not the time for theatrics. She wouldn't allow her feelings to obscure this moment.

Drawing in a breath that felt as if it originated in her toes and traveled the network of her body to its exhale, Kenna cleared her head. She channeled neutrality, imagined cool nothingness flowing through her, flushing out anything that might have prevented her from listening to the impending story with anything less than an impartial ear.

Heart and mind empty, she beheld Dayton, viewing him without the lens of all of his associations. He was just a man, seated opposite her in a diner, with a story to tell. She was just there to collect the facts.

"Are you going to speak or is it your goal to keep us here half the night?"

It sounded so very different from something she would've said under normal circumstances. Nevertheless, it elicited a response.

"It was a dark and stormy night."

"If you're going to mock the gravity of this by quoting classics, I'm leaving." She rose but before she had a chance to walk away he spoke once more.

"Sit."

The harshness of the 't' alone was enough to send her scrambling into the booth.

"I kid you not. It was, in fact, dark and stormy. There was no sky that day, just a blanket of gray clouds. The kind of menacing overcast that tricks you into thinking it's dinnertime but you look at the clock and noon hasn't even rolled around. And yet it hadn't rained."

"Terrible weather. I get it."

"Tyler didn't attend Ponderosa, which made tracking him a little more difficult. I relied on Jasmine for that. She was cutting our visits short so as not to arouse suspicion. I decided to let my irritation fuel something more productive. You may not approve of my working definition here." He flashed a smile, one that faded before it reached his dark eyes. "I followed her to Tyler's place one afternoon, stayed well beyond when she'd left. He didn't leave his apartment that day. So I kept going back. I made note of things, learned his schedule. All of this in order to determine an appropriate time to intercept."

"You could've knocked on his door like a normal person."

"And risk him calling the police?"

"At least then maybe he'd still be alive."

His gaze pinned her to the vinyl. Kenna was a petrified butterfly. Shriveled and defenseless.

There went her calculated demeanor.

"Isn't there something in the Bible about passing prejudgment?"

"Minus the prefix, sure."

He ignored the mouthy remark, continuing, "He worked at this sad electronics store. That's where he was heading that evening. Tyler always parked a few blocks up. I'd planned to confront him when he got out of the car."

Something subtle shifted in his face. She glanced at his scars, those rippled white lines. Marks that signified one's survival and another's death.

"How exactly did you plan to keep him away? Gentle persuasion clearly doesn't suit you. Money seems too Hollywood." Kenna couldn't stop herself from reasoning aloud. He was the 1,000-piece puzzle she'd been tirelessly tweezing into place, the final image becoming clearer by the day. "A violent confrontation would've been too messy so that leaves … the tape."

"Recorded solely for the purpose of blackmailing them both. Using it against Tyler was contingent upon him being a caring boyfriend. Based on Jasmine's texts, he was."

Her forearms grew taut. Skin stretched paper thin.

"Have you ever gone through my phone?"

"When you began studying under me, I believe I told you something to the effect of, 'Don't ask questions you don't want to know the answer to.'"

"You're right. Asking is pointless. I should save us both the trouble and assume the worst."

"As I was saying, the storm seemed like an empty threat. Not long after I started tailing Tyler, one raindrop hit the windshield. Another, another. Soon, it was pouring. Coming down in sheets. Thunder like you've never heard. Lightning flashes that would put even the most alert drivers on edge. It was cinematic, really."

"Yes, well, the world is God's stage. Go on."

"I was too close to him. I don't know if the weather or my motivation was to blame."

Silence stretched between them.

"So, that's it? You were tailgating, hit his bumper, sent him off the road?"

"Possibly."

"You were there," she enunciated.

"Physically, yes. Consciously, no."

"What the hell are you—" she broke off, realizing at once what he meant.

"I passed out going 70 in a thunderstorm. Tyler died and I didn't. My survival was nothing short of a miracle but it left me with a great deal of guilt. I stopped the—" He paused and she was eaten alive by the mystery that hid behind his censure. "I stopped looking for girls, retreated into myself for a time. I wanted to seek confessional on a consistent basis but I was only able to drag myself there on Christmas Eve. Sorry excuse for a Catholic, I am. Deep down, I know no amount of confession will erase what I've done or the way I feel. The way I *am*. I was born broken."

Whatever Kenna thought she might have felt upon hearing his side of things was void. She didn't know what to feel and as a result she felt everything all at once.

Tyler's death had been an accident.

Dayton had been telling the truth all along.

That knowledge, in the white fluorescence of the diner, made him a little less monstrous.

18

EVERY VERSION

Dayton

At the practice, he and Kenna carried on with business as usual. Marriage had not changed their working dynamic. It had changed little else, really.

The nameplate on her desk read, 'Ms. O'Callaghan; reception.' Her agreement to their arrangement was nothing short of reluctant; he wasn't going to press his luck by quarreling over minor details like whether she'd update a silly little plaque.

He had her. That was all that mattered.

In spite of the promise he'd made to her on the O'Callaghans' orchard, she wasn't softening to their new union. Dayton kept telling himself she'd come around. Perhaps a cooling-off period was in order. She continued helping him with his work and, though it benefitted her too, he was grateful for her constant presence amid the scientific field that had originally brought them together.

Free of classes for the summer, she fully embraced his schedule. They opened together in the mornings and locked up in the evenings. The academic zeal that characterized her final stint of undergrad and her early days at the practice was gone, replaced by a wariness acquired by the virtue of sticking around much longer than the girls who'd come before her. Rather than staying behind and bombarding him with questions or observations, Kenna often rushed off to a singing gig and wouldn't return home until well into the night. It was painfully obvious that she did this for the distraction more than the money.

Dayton worked through lunch most days, door shut, but he wasn't poring over patient files. He reviewed the manuscript that started taking shape shortly after he was hired at Ponderosa. His contribution to the realm of psychiatry.

A couple years prior, he had contacted some bigwig academics with publishing connections. They told him he'd better think twice about putting something 'of this nature' to press. According to them, no publisher in their right mind would touch it and, hypothetically, if they did, the American Psychological Association would have a field day. Where was the informed consent? Forget about beneficence, justice, or anything else.

The second Shane Sanders was indicted, he'd personally publish the book. No matter if it was his ruin.

This was his legacy.

A knock came at the door. There were no barriers between them and yet Kenna's politeness never failed. He still found it endearing. Dayton switched to his decoy files long before the door creaked inward. He'd become an expert at the swift maneuver as a result of the occasions Kenna had stumbled into the living room in the middle of the night, checking on him during the hours when he most valued his privacy. With her living in the house, it had become increasingly difficult to work on his book, which was the primary reason he had taken to doing so at the office whenever private moments could be stolen.

Her warm hand cupped his bicep, less out of affection and

more as a way to get his attention. He welcomed the touch regardless. "I have to get going. Early reception. Will you be alright?"

"I'll manage."

He suspected she was asking out of duty rather than courtesy and the notion pained him. It tore the veil away and revealed their true nature. Kenna, a caged bird. He, her keeper. She was testing his established boundaries. Would she be able to leave outside of their usual hours? Pain seized his jaw, as if it were being slowly sutured shut with steel wire.

"Go," he forced himself to say. "They won't pay if you're late."

His throat tensed as he watched her scurry out of the room. It dismayed him that they had progressed linearly in the public eye with their marriage, while the interior of their relationship was regressing. Glancing at his wedding band, Dayton siphoned a steadying breath before returning his focus to the laptop.

He had work to do.

Kenna

She'd been offered a number of gigs in Portland, all of which she refused. Though she had gained experience behind the wheel, she didn't trust herself to make the nearly one-hour drive.

Since their return from Syracuse, she'd begun booking wedding receptions. Time away from Dayton was the most appealing factor but, Kenna realized, she also missed performing. She missed the solid feel of her guitar's wooden neck cradled in her hands. And, even though it seemed a touch narcissistic, she missed standing on a stage and holding the attention of everyone in a room, a bar, a party.

She'd never been artistically inclined but the vibrations of her vocal chords were an art all their own.

Playing the receptions had become essential to her everyday survival. The music provided breathing room. It gave her a surplus of the oxygen that was stripped from her lungs whenever she set foot in the house on Fairbrook, whose walls tightened upon her entry.

Too much idle time there was dangerous.

Kenna pushed it out of her mind. She didn't allow herself to dwell on such things while she was strumming and vocalizing the soundtrack to someone else's happily ever after.

These weddings were so very different from her own. Filled with genuine feeling and laughter. Family and friends who supported the newlyweds.

No one objected or complicated things.

The weight of the guitar resting against her body calmed her as she referenced the set list taped on the stage. Many of the songs were horribly cliché but Kenna wasn't there to judge. This was her psych ward time, a few hours when she emptied her mind and played along to whatever was required of her. She was safe in that white room, with the guitar as her straitjacket.

During a slow song, her attention kept drifting to a table on the left side of the room, where a woman in a violet dress had not taken her eyes off Kenna. A sick feeling wormed its way into her gut as she feared the worst. Was she another Polaroid girl, warning her about her husband's maleficent ways?

That paranoia, however slight, greased the wheels of her mind and soon it was racing. Hallucinations taunted her as she fought to finish the song. Kenna stared in bewilderment as the woman's features continuously morphed to reflect the girls she had failed to track down. Dakota, Freya, Giselle, Harmony.

Were they dead? Alive?

Had they moved on from all of this or were their minds forever changed, a terrifying maze from which there was no escape?

Kenna dropped to her knees, arms shrouding her head. She didn't realize she was screaming until her throat started stinging. Darkness fell over her vision and suddenly there were no lights, no sound, only the weightless sensation of being carried away.

. . .

Hours later, she awoke on the couch. Her hazy vision cleared and revealed the wooden beams that lined the ceiling of their home.

"Can we talk about what happened tonight?"

The voice jarred Kenna into complete consciousness. Dayton sat on the edge of the armchair, hands steepled as if she were in critical condition. She patted her arms and legs in search of injury, but came up empty. On the surface, she seemed fine. She remembered everything clearly. Forcefully, almost, as if she'd been struck over the head with the memory.

Hallucinations. Fainting. Being picked up.

It was only then she realized whose arms she had been in, and that gave way to a chilling realization.

"You followed me tonight. To my gig. How did you even know where I was?"

"Smartphones have GPS. Don't view this as some malignant attack on your privacy." Dayton smoothed his hands over his pants, as if to regroup himself. "I'm worried about your headspace. You ran off to New York without a second thought … you could use some looking after."

"Why don't you let me worry about my headspace."

"It's my professional opinion that you should be seen. The hospital, a therapist, online counseling. Whatever you prefer."

"As much as I respect your opinion, *doctor*, the decision is ultimately mine."

"I won't tolerate your hostility."

"You bred it. Now you have to raise it."

"Goddamn it, Kenna."

On reflex, she crossed herself, knowing he wouldn't.

Dayton's phone rang.

"Dr. Merino." A smile. Nothing grand, but there was warmth to it. "I apologize. Personal calls are rare." A pause. "She is."

He handed the phone to Kenna, which she answered with suspicion. "Hello?"

"Is he still roughing you up?"

She'd scarcely registered who was speaking when she pushed the answer out. "No."

"Good. We'll send Taryn and Oona, whenever you're ready."

"Fallon, what—"

The line went dead.

She made the connection instantly. "They have my number. Why did you leave yours?"

"Before we left, I told Fallon the girls are welcome to visit anytime."

"Oh, and it didn't cross your mind to run it by me first? Or my mother?" As Kenna's heart wrenched, she wondered when their love would stop feeling like this; dominoes of sheet glass and she was caught between each one as they shattered.

"Your mother is bordering on comatose. She spends the whole day in her bedroom. I doubt she'll notice anyone's missing."

"Tell me, when did my family become so important to you? Was it during the eight months you withheld my father's death?"

"You clearly wanted nothing to do with them at the time. I thought I was protecting you."

Her glare held him hostage as searing words fell from her lips. "I used to think it was your cold heart that made you so dangerous, but now you've made it quite clear it's your unending ability to justify."

Ignoring her comment, he said, "I'd like to take you to the hospital."

Kenna considered the impracticality of conducting a psych evaluation in the ER. The swishing curtains and mumbled questions.

"And if I reveal something incriminating?"

"Then I'll accept the repercussions, without argument." He held her hand, thumb tracing the ridges of her palms. "And I'll relish that my punishment was at the hand of someone I love."

Never did it fail to blow her mind how easily they breezed from tension to shouting to calm affection.

She jerked her hand away, rising from the couch. "No. I'm not going anywhere except to bed."

Pacing toward the bedroom, the pounds, sleep, and friends she'd lost as a result of this relationship weighed down every step. Her pride, that hallmark of masculinity, was still intact. She needed nothing else.

"If you keep pressuring me to get help, I'll push back, and it will ruin you. And, despite your cute little speech a minute ago, I know that is the furthest thing from what you want. You wouldn't have corralled me into this marriage otherwise." Kenna stood in the mouth of the hall, all the poise of a cinematic villain. "Good night, darling."

19

SAY YOUR PRAYERS

Dayton

Late evening sun shone through the stained glass windows in St. James. Light pierced the squares of red, yellow, blue, giving them the appearance of jewels.

Dayton zoned out on the architectural finery, unaware of anyone or anything around him. It was only through Kenna's discrete prompting that he managed to mime proper Mass etiquette.

"Say your prayers," she whispered.

He bowed his head, the polished stone floor replacing his view of the artful windows. Strictly speaking, he didn't pray. He filtered all of his thoughts until all that remained reflected his most earnest desire: Kenna seeking counseling.

He wasn't sure what exactly had happened at her gig since he'd arrived shortly before she collapsed on the stage. All he knew was that the incident had spooked her. With times as dark as they were, he couldn't afford to have her in such a state.

He needed her mellow, collected, brandishing that razor-sharp intellect he loved like a battle-ax.

For all the choices that led him here, it would ultimately be her decision if he came out on the other side of things. When the truth came out and Kenna discovered that she could, in fact, testify against him, she'd decide his fate.

"Amen," he mumbled.

She squeezed his hand but he hardly spared her a sidelong glance before returning his attention to the stained glass. Dayton had a plan in place to ease her into the idea of therapy. Inwardly, he begged for her receptiveness.

Kenna

Things were strained at home that evening, though the same could've been said for the preceding days. Despite this, they still carried out their pre-wedding promises: Dayton attended Mass with her and she accompanied him on runs.

There was an emptiness to those duties now. They were going through the motions, nothing more.

Talking had almost become an old pastime.

Kenna wished to speak to him, but Dayton proved more firm in his resolve. His silence was like an electric fence. Coaxing him out of it could prove fatal. She kept her distance, held her tongue, as he retreated further and further into himself.

She perched on the edge of the bed, tuning her guitar in anticipation of her next performance. Occasionally, her thumb stroked the strings to gauge whether the proper sound had been achieved. Once she was satisfied, she played through one of her favorite Of Monsters and Men songs. As she strummed, she missed the familiar weight of her Saint Rose bracelet. She'd practically turned the house upside down and had never found it.

Kenna became so lost in the music, she failed to notice the man looming in the doorway.

"What is that?"

Heart rate mellowing out, she managed a response. "Sinking Man."

Dayton nodded, appearing deep in thought. "I like it. It's melancholic." Digging in his back pocket, he tossed something at her, which she swiftly caught. Then, he met her eyes. "You left this on the bookcase."

The motion of the phone being thrown through the air brought the home screen to life momentarily, long enough for her to notice a message from an unsaved number.

> I've been thinking about what you said…
> can you still help me?

Suddenly, she remembered the offer she'd extended to Jasmine and felt rotten for not reaching out herself. Hurt lashed at Kenna's chest. They hadn't even known each other and yet Jasmine had gone out of her way to bring attention to an evil of which Kenna was already painfully aware; an evil, she realized, she harbored no chance of escaping because she'd become a part of it. Every sinister act committed by Dayton, every indiscretion, lie, breach of ethics or morality, it all twisted around her heart, her mind, as if that guilt rested equally with her.

Returning a videotape was the absolute least she could do to combat that villainy.

"I'm going to take the garbage out."

"Okay," Kenna said, not knowing why she had replied or why he had announced such a mundane task.

She didn't linger on the peculiarity of the statement for long. Her mind soon latched onto more important details, like the fact that she knew precisely how long it took him to bring the trash around the side of the house. Eschewing her guitar, she dropped to the floor.

Once upon a time, her fingers would've trembled as she peeled back the rug. Her anxiety would've piqued at the time constraint. But Kenna O'Callaghan-Merino acted only with surety.

That frightening confidence soon abandoned her.

As she lifted away the last plank, her stomach lurched at the sight below. All that had once been there was gone. A small, brown spider crawled around within the space.

Hastily righting the boards, it occurred to her with a terrifying certainty, the front door had never opened. Dayton hadn't gone outside.

Too late, she heard footsteps.

Strong arms locked around Kenna and, though her instinct was to struggle, she made no sound for she was far too stunned. Her brain couldn't make sense of what was happening but her body knew enough to fight. No matter how much she struggled against Dayton, elbows jabbing and legs kicking, he did not budge.

"This isn't how I'd planned it. Please forgive me."

A smokescreen descended over her vision. Everything went foggy and gray and soon faded to black.

20

WHIDBEY

Kenna

ovement jostled Kenna awake.

She struggled with the heaviness of her eyelids. When she managed to open them, like the agonizingly slow unveiling of a curtain, she was met with darkness. It was black as pitch save for a pair of headlights illuminating the road. The beams were about as useful as a flashlight in the unfathomable dark, revealing only what lay a short distance ahead and not stretching beyond the road's shoulder.

"Good. You're up."

Though it shouldn't have, the voice startled her. Sinister shadows obscured Dayton's face as he manned the wheel. This must have been a nightmare. A horrible dream. Yes, that was it. Except when Kenna shut her eyes and opened them once more, the same grim scene greeted her.

"Tell me why you were rifling through my things."

Fractals of what transpired—of whatever had delivered them to this moment—came back to her. She remembered playing guitar, the itch of the rug against her fingertips, the heft of the floor-boards. The crawl space.

Slowly, she said, "It was empty."

"Never mind that. Answer my question."

Her voice turned accusatory. "You *grabbed* me. You grabbed me and held me down, and I couldn't breathe." Through gritted teeth, Kenna demanded, "What did you do to me?"

"Pressure point. I sent you into a state of unconsciousness."

"Unconsciousness," she repeated. His casual mention of it was more alarming than usual.

"Minimize your disbelief. I didn't try to kill you. This wouldn't have been such a dramatic shock had you just gone to bed instead of nosing around. I'd planned to carry you out to the car before you woke up. Tell you the truth, I don't know why I had one iota of faith in that plan." He muttered under his breath, "Always expediting things. Making it impossible to think clearly."

Plans. She circled back to her awareness that they were in the car. The dash proclaimed it was just shy of four in the morning. They drove over a slight divot and the distinct vibration of crossing a bridge filled her ears. Water spanned either side of the roadway, twinkling in the dark.

"Where are we going?"

He shot her a shockingly emotive look. One that, in the span of a few seconds, insinuated he'd rather drive them off that bridge than admit their destination.

"On the honeymoon we didn't have."

They zipped past a sign that said *Deception Pass State Park* and her heartbeat ratcheted up as her toes curled and teeth clenched. She didn't recognize the name, but that didn't necessarily mean anything. Oregon was a fairly large state and she had only explored a small fraction of it. Unless they had crossed some border she was unaware of while she'd been unconscious. Perhaps they were in California. Washington. Kenna eliminated Canada with a great deal of certainty. She didn't think they'd been on the road long enough to reach it and then there was the issue of a passport, a document she did not possess.

But regardless of where they were, not for one second did she believe they were en route to a honeymoon. Dayton had knocked her out. He'd caught her peering into his hidey-hole. A tremendous sinking feeling settled over her and Kenna realized that he'd likely read the text from Jasmine. His leaving her alone in the bedroom had been a test and she had failed. Suddenly, it all felt like a nasty trick.

The visual of the empty crawl space plagued her as her heart rate competed with the speedometer.

With frightening clarity, Kenna recalled the first time she'd accepted a ride from him, that fateful day in the Roth's parking lot. Her fear, while minimal then, had only gained more and more validity as time went on.

She ached for the days when she'd merely feared him, for now terror weighed down her bones in the passenger seat as she fleetingly wondered if this would be her last car ride. Her last glimpse of the moon and the stars.

It was a grotesque thing to contemplate but she forced herself to accept it was not beyond the realm of possibility.

They soon arrived at a cabin that was perched along the shore. Gravel crunched beneath the Taycan's tires. She found herself on high alert as Dayton moved the gear shift into park. He got out and migrated to the trunk to collect their things, she presumed. Her knuckles turned white as she gripped the door handle. If she ran, how far would she make it before he brought her to the ground and dragged her back to this very spot? He was a seasoned runner, after all.

Kenna jumped slightly when he opened the passenger door and she looked up at his dour face in the shadowy night.

"Let's get you inside," Dayton said, gently guiding her by the arm into the cabin as if he hadn't put her to sleep with his bare hands hours earlier.

It was a balancing act he performed startlingly well. Care and concern following on the heels of malicious behavior. He'd given her tea after he drugged her. Now, he tucked her into an unfamiliar bed and pressed a soft kiss to her forehead.

"Get some rest. Tomorrow, we'll start fresh."

She noticed something he'd been doing all along: speaking to her in commands rather than questions. Dayton was trying to domesticate her like the gentle lamb for which he constantly mistook her. What would it take for him to see she was a wolf in sheep's clothing? Beneath her glamorous exterior she sported long, sharp canines and claws.

Nestled under the covers, she stared out the window at the dark nothingness and the Polaroid girls lingered at the frayed edges of her consciousness. Were she in any danger, she wanted to think they'd have her back. That one text, call, or email might save her. Even in her current haze of exhaustion, she wasn't gullible enough to buy into those thoughts.

It was possible she had made enemies of every one of them. They knew she was carrying on with Dayton in some manner and it required little imagination to fill in the sordid details.

As she succumbed to sleep, she dreamed of a pack of wolves, howling and running together by the light of a fat, yellow moon. One of them lagged behind, forgotten.

The wolves were gone. The day had come.

She pushed herself to a sitting position, hand shooting to cradle her neck which was stiff from uninterrupted sleep.

Quiet suffused the cabin. A twisted blanket had been left on the couch and she reasoned that must have been where Dayton had slept as there was only one bedroom.

A quick poke around revealed that Kenna was alone. She twisted the ring around her finger and wondered why she wore it, why he'd left her here.

If he was coming back.

A note lying on the kitchen counter addressed her last concern. She picked it up, reading silently.

Grab the wine beside the fridge
and meet me on the dock at nightfall.

If his idea of a honeymoon was abandoning her in a cabin in the woods, then she was glad she'd run off to New York after the wedding. She kicked herself for coming home with him. Deep down, she knew the real reason she'd returned was not her love for him but rather because all of this felt dreadfully unfinished. Her conversations with the Polaroid girls and her attempts to decode her wicked husband and the crown jewel at the heart of this madness: the murder of Lacey Greene.

Whoever would've thought a dead girl would be responsible for a marriage.

Kenna was alarmed when she caught sight of the clock beside the refrigerator. It was well into the afternoon. She could not remember the last time she'd slept so long. Though, she knew, it was likely a result of the prior night's events.

She performed a more in-depth sweep of the cabin and discovered her cell phone was missing. She didn't find Dayton's phone, either, and there was no landline. No computer. No radio. No way to connect with the outside world.

Kenna wondered if the lack of technology was an intentional choice by the owners of the cabin—people liked to unplug when in nature—or if the items had been stowed away in the trunk of the sports car as an insurance policy.

It was then she realized, standing in the middle of the small cabin with no way to seek help, she'd been kidnapped.

Maybe Dayton had adopted one of those complexes criminals got once they had a few minor crimes under their belt. The feeling that nothing could touch them. Truthfully, she felt he'd long considered himself untouchable.

This was a man who, on a daily basis, grappled with the possibility that he might be convicted for murder and yet, in the meantime, he still carried on his days as a respectable member of society. He was a doctor, a pillar of the community. By that logic, it was no wonder Reynolds' lieutenant wanted him to focus his search elsewhere.

She was hit with the overwhelming need to sit as she dwelled on the subject. Her knees had gone loose and it became difficult to stand. It seemed like it had been another lifetime when she and Dayton had last spoken of Lacey Greene.

A sickening realization surfaced. Kenna had not inquired about it because, though she'd long suspected his guilt, confirmation of his action would be too devastating.

"Stop," she said, nails digging into her scalp.

Spending the day panicking about her apparent kidnapping or her husband's innocence was unwise. She had to conserve her energy for nightfall and in order to do that, she needed a distraction from her overactive thoughts.

Weathered copies of mass market bestsellers lined the TV console's shelves. Hanging beside the TV was an illustrated map of Whidbey Island, Washington. Kenna wondered if that was where they were or if it was an unrelated piece of decor.

Snatching a title at random, she took it to the couch and, upon cracking it open, the cover page ripped off and drifted to the floor.

Kenna closely monitored the passage of day to night, glancing out the exposed windows every half hour. As the afternoon stretched into the evening, the book may as well have been written in Latin. Anxiety stripped away her comprehension.

She proceeded with extreme caution when it came time to meet Dayton. To ensure her drink had not been laced with GHB or any other mind-altering drug, Kenna did two things.

One, she selected a corked bottle of wine if only to eliminate the chance that it had been tampered with. Two, she selected a pair of stemmed glasses from the cupboard and, even though they were bone dry, she washed them not once, not twice, but three times in case her husband swabbed their rims with a substance-soaked tissue.

One could never be too careful when they were married to Dr. Dayton Edward Merino.

Captor of minds, keeper of hearts.

Despite it being the end of June, there was a chill in the air as Kenna stepped out of the cabin, basket of drinks in tow. With one hand, she clutched the thin throw blanket that was draped around her to ensure she didn't lose it.

Her bare feet met the worn wood of the dock and each step toward Dayton sent her stomach into knots. He waited for her at the water's edge, lighting candles as if the very thing they stood upon weren't flammable.

Was that his plan? To burn them alive?

Silently, she called upon God and prayed for the strength to steel herself against those harmful thoughts.

A small smile graced his lips as he noticed her approaching. Extinguishing the match, he lowered himself to a sitting position. Kenna stopped short a few paces behind him. Nerves overcame her that—aside from her previously established fears—made little sense.

"It's beautiful out here, isn't it? Peaceful."

She scanned the landscape. Creatures howled within the dense forest wall beyond the shoreline. Silver moonlight glistened on the still water of Puget Sound. No streetlights or sign of civilization. Just the two of them, enshrouded in darkness, surrounded by the natural world. It was, dare she say, romantic.

Kenna sat down beside him, placing the ice bucket between them. "It is. I've never seen anything like this before."

"I'm sure you've seen some sort of breathtaking scenery. Your family's land is quite extensive."

She drew her knees to her chest. "I meant that I've never seen a body of water this big. It's surreal, and also kind of terrifying."

"Do you have a phobia of water?" His face went tight, as if it were being pulled by an invisible force.

"I'm not afraid of it, per se. I'm afraid of the power it has. People put blind faith in it. They dive in and assume they'll resurface. But then Mother Nature asserts dominance and swallows them whole. And that person is gone … forever. The water doesn't change. This is its stasis."

"Are we still talking about the Sound?"

"Must everything have psychological undertones?"

Undertones were, in fact, in Kenna's comment. But if Dayton wanted to kidnap and drag her out to the sticks, then obstinacy was fair game.

Tension ruled his features, emphasizing the lines around his mouth. Brows, downcast. "Why were you in the crawl space?"

He posed the question in a way that suggested everything—whatever it may have been—depended upon her answer.

"I was looking for Jasmine's tape."

Dayton stared at her, his eyes far more insidious in the dark. "You meant to return it?"

She nodded and showed no outward fear while her mind played a scene in which he held her head under the Sound until her water-logged lungs took their final breath.

Terror crept across her brain and she felt its movement, like a spider crawling along someone's skin.

He captured her chin and brought her back to the present. The darkness in his eyes intensified. Kenna had looked into those black pools a thousand times yet she still found their depthless quality haunting. The silent but familiar demand of his fingers on her face and their slow dance, that rhythmic, infinitesimal movement transformed the scene.

No longer was she trapped in a nightmare.

Gazing upon the shimmering black water, she understood this

was a Grimm fairy tale. She danced beside the dark sea with her prince—who'd long tempted her with his wicked ways. Their chests drew closer and their hearts competed with one another. Something in that moment told her that was exactly where she was supposed to be.

Had she not become just as wicked?

"We could have everything."

The sentiment startled her. It was as if he'd gained access to her thoughts. She easily read what was etched into Dayton's face. He craved acceptance of the elusive thing that had always hung between them: trust. Her throat felt impossibly thick, as if its lining had been replaced with tree bark, and her voice took on a creaky quality when she spoke. All she managed to say was his name, but a plea laced itself in those two syllables.

"Dayton."

Sweeping her hair off her shoulder, he pitched his voice lower. "Why did you seek me out? Why did you knock on my office door?"

"You were the best choice for my mentorship."

He seemed dissatisfied by the answer.

"No, lamb. You came to me because you knew I had the power to help you achieve your goals. You came to me because you needed me." He traced the edge of her jaw. His touch was sharp against her skin. The tip of a knife. "Now, I need you."

"Why me?"

It was not the first time she'd presented him with the question. Despite the dark spell she was under, she thought it necessary to ask again.

"I love you like I've loved nothing else and, if I cannot have you by my side, I won't survive any of this." Dayton stroked her cheek in reverence. "I need Saint Kenna to see me through."

The nickname triggered a flurry of memories. The girl she used to be. The girl she had become. And, in one violent motion, something snapped in her brain and her remembrance ceased.

Bringing herself closer to him, Kenna spoke against his mouth, words burning like flames. "I'm no saint."

Dayton did not claim her mouth. He devoured it. It was a feeling to which she'd grown accustomed, that of suffocation. She became lightheaded and wondered if the scanty snatches of oxygen she stole from him were solely responsible for her consciousness.

Though they starred in a twisted version of a honeymoon, their clothes were torn off without ceremony. There was nothing to consummate.

Passion was absent from their affair. Rather, it was too weak a word. What unfolded between them beneath the midnight sky was feral, a sickening hunger that ratcheted with every nip and scratch.

He pinned Kenna to the rough wooden planks and her hair cascaded off the side of the dock, the ends lilting in the inky water. Her back chafed against the wood and she felt a concentrated sting in several places. Splinters.

Her fingers grazed the pacemaker embedded under his skin and she was reminded of how delicate his foothold was in this life —and how there was nothing delicate about the way he lived.

His hand gloved her neck, shattering her affectionate touch. She had been foolish to pet a beast.

Dayton's thrusts turned slow and punishing as he held her gaze. His palm compressed her throat. She should've focused what little energy she had on screaming but the delicious rush of oxytocin demanded her silence.

"Is there any part of you I shouldn't trust?"

Her sex, for welcoming him without reservation. Her heart, for loving him with reckless abandon. Her mind, for thinking she could decode him.

They were all reasons she should not trust herself, and so she offered none of them to him.

"No."

His body went rigid above hers. As soon as his lustful paralysis cleared, he freed her from the shackles of his weight.

"I won't be so cruel as to ask the same of you. But tell me, what do you see when you look in my eyes?"

She studied him and decided to answer honestly.

"Misery," she breathed.

"None of my love is reflected there?"

"Not tonight."

It was true. Usually, there was love there, flitting around the edges of his black irises. A golden edge of pure emotion which she'd once thought him incapable of producing. Something had possessed him when he had dug his fingers into her neck and she suspected it lurked behind those changed eyes.

"Want to know what I see in yours?" Dayton asked, tracing her collarbone. "That terror-stricken look of a deer that's staring down the barrel of a shotgun."

"Then I pray there are no guns here, doctor."

His touch coasted over her shoulder and along her arm. "Oh, but there's love there too. You've become quite the little masochist."

Kenna wanted to argue her brain was the real masochist, with its incessant need to understand things that were better left alone.

Two ghostly fingers reached out and shut her eyelids and a tiredness like she'd never known overtook her. The shadowy, shapeless limbs of sleep cradled her as the sounds of the world petered out and there was only the small fire in her lungs and the lulling cadence of her gentle breath.

21

WILDERNESS

Dayton

The sun's golden warmth coupled with a light breeze glancing off his skin ushered Dayton awake. Eyelids peeling back slowly, his vision came into focus while studying Kenna's bare, sleeping form.

She had all but passed out the night before and he worried that moving her might have stirred up the resentment he had so skillfully tempered. They'd slept on the dock, naked beneath a blanket of stars, one with nature.

Dayton drank in the serene quality of her face, hoping, praying, wishing that this new day wouldn't erase yesterday's progress.

His chest pinched at the slight bruising across her neck. Knocking her unconscious hadn't been part of his plan but when he'd seen her gazing into the open pit in the floor, the space that had housed so many figurative ghosts, he'd felt he had no choice. Adrenaline went into overdrive.

Just like …

Kenna's eyes fluttered open, wincing against the light. She

scrambled to a sitting position, forearm welded to her breasts when she registered her state of undress.

"Here," he said, handing over his shirt, "you can at least wear this inside."

After pulling it over her head, her lips parted in confusion as she looked around. "Where's the rest of our clothes?"

"The water, more than likely. Either that or a curious but non-aggressive bear paid us a visit." Dayton grimaced at the taste of his stale mouth. He stood without a stitch of clothing and couldn't help but smile when Kenna turned her head. Nodding in the direction of the cabin, he said, "Come along, we're due for a hike."

Kenna

Whatever happened on the dock must have been of incredible significance considering Kenna was traipsing through the Washington wilderness with the dark doctor.

Hours had passed since they'd entered the trail and Dayton had said little else besides giving an occasional direction. They were surrounded by so much beauty that the relative silence between them was welcome.

She lingered a few feet behind, admiring the muscular strain of his calves. Sweat bonded his gray shirt to his back. His medical bracelet jostled with every step.

The gunmetal jewelry transported her to the 5K. Kenna had largely been in the dark about his behavior, but she'd feared for her life when they set out among hundreds of other runners. A fear that escalated upon Dayton's collapse and imploded once she realized he hadn't worn his potentially life-saving bracelet. In the ambulance, the moment he'd squeezed her hand solidified something terrifying for her.

She had not wanted him to die.

In spite of everything, that hadn't changed.

Despite the joy he brought her, the reminder that her life may have been at risk never strayed very far. Their relationship was like that of an animal trainer and a bear. Kenna convinced herself they had a connection others couldn't comprehend and he was capable of being tame for her. But no amount of bonding would eliminate his basic instincts.

Without warning, she could become his prey.

She jumped back as Dayton whirled around, their moves executed in an almost choreographed manner.

"How do you fare with heights?"

"What, you're conducting a survey on my fears now?" Kenna's hands found her hips as her heart rate steadied itself. "Last night, you asked if I was afraid of water. Do you have some kind of hidden objective for this trip? Are you hoping to find out what my limits are?"

"I understand your paranoia, given the circumstances under which you were brought here. We're taking this trip because I want to spend time with you. That is the only reason."

Her stomach lurched at his last sentence. It sounded as if he was trying to convince himself rather than her.

Dayton headed up a hill but, upon realizing she hadn't moved, stopped and called down to her. "Come on. We've made it this far. The view from the top is supposed to be incredible."

Feet rooted to the dirt, she glanced in either direction, bemoaning the desolation that most people found peaceful. Although, those people hadn't willingly hiked into the heart of a forest with a potential killer.

Physiologically, Kenna sensed danger; yet when she took in the sight of his distant face, she only felt comfort. A thrilling curiosity zipped through her. Her body was engaged in fight or flight but, like an unreliable narrator, her poisoned brain had fired those signals. She ignored the warning and caught up with Dayton.

She had always trusted her mind over her body.

Trekking up the hillside winded Kenna. Her lung capacity had deteriorated since trading her beloved bike for the station wagon.

Muscles blazing, she peered at Dayton. She wondered how much of a strain a hike of this caliber had on his heart. It reeked of reckless behavior, even with her accompanying him.

The view was breathtaking. A cinematic panorama of nature extending in every direction.

Dayton lowered himself onto the hill's rocky ledge, downing water and motioning for her to join him. They sat atop that massive rock and gazed out onto the most beautiful landscape she had ever seen.

One thought refused to leave her. A thought that dispelled the magical moment and prompted her to acknowledge the man at her side. With the slightest bit of courage, she formed a question that needed no explanation.

"Did you do it?"

"Yes."

That whispered word contained the weight of the world. It all pressed down on her at once. Crushing, compressing, constraining. Heartbreak and repulsion and dread threaded through her bones. And yet disbelief did not surface, for a small part of her had known the truth all along.

She found herself wanting to say something while simultaneously being incapable of speech. Dayton didn't have to answer and yet he had. No longer did she have to wonder or deliberate.

He had done it.

Anyone else in her position might have been worried; sitting beside a freshly confessed murderer on a boulder's ledge. But the man next to her showed no sign of anger or preeminent violence, nor did Kenna fear that he may push her to the forest floor below. For she understood all that he'd yet to say would hurt far worse than that fall.

Scanning the treetops, he said, "I didn't mean to harm her. It all happened so fast."

Her body no longer felt like her own. It was invaded by some alien force. Unshed tears and nausea and cold sweat tested the restraint of every cell.

She found her voice. "Harm her? You *killed* her."

Dayton shot her a look that was nothing short of apologetic and she found it mad, that expression, like he was a child who'd spilled a glass of milk at the dinner table. He maintained that look as she shouted. "You killed her. You killed her!"

He made no motion to stop her and so she rode out the wave of hysterics until she rendered herself mute.

"Every morning when I wake up, all I feel is remorse."

"Then why did you do it?"

"It was impulsive."

Gingerly, Kenna touched his wrist and spoke words that terrified her. "People come into your office and bare their souls to you. Let me be that for you, for the sake of your body and mind. Let's start with the why."

His gaze traveled toward the sky before dipping down and meeting her own. "Because of you."

"Sorry?"

"You're the reason."

Everything collapsed inside of her. Bones turned to dust. Heart shriveled until it crumbled to bits. To think, he was blaming his actions on her … well, it was unthinkable.

"She showed up looking like she'd escaped something out of a horror story. In a way, she had. She'd been chained up in Sanders' basement for days. She was hysterical when she caught me on the street. Crying, filthy, bruised. It wasn't long before you were due for your shift."

She knew from experience that Dayton wasn't much of a crier but one might think rehashing the story of how he took someone's life might have been one such occasion.

No matter how remorseful he'd claimed to be, his austerity gave nothing away.

"Imagine what would've happened had I invited her inside. You show up and see her sitting in the waiting room. You see her like *that*. The way she was …" His voice trailed off, each syllable softer than the last.

If you invited her inside, she'd still be alive. Her molars clamped on the side of her tongue to keep the comment at bay.

"Now look at me and tell me you would've reacted in a way that was anything short of hysterical. We both know you would have been all over me in an instant. Accusing, interrogating. You're simply *incapable* of waiting for an explanation." He hung his head and looked in her direction, but not at her. "It's always in your eyes, that judgment. All I ever wanted was your love."

"You have it."

It was a truth she did not want to relinquish in such a grim moment. Like always, she needed the rest of the story and saw no alternative to push him onward.

"I told her to meet me around back. I'd already made up my mind at that point."

Kenna's stomach lurched as his sidelong gaze bore into her. In her 23 years, it was the most evil thing she had ever heard: confessing the decision to take someone else's life.

"Following her wouldn't have looked good for passersby. Of course, in the moment, I didn't account for the traffic cameras. I couldn't have. My brain was firing on adrenaline and fear and a thousand other things that, if you asked me now, I still couldn't name." His hand braced his brows, thumb and pointer finger acting as a divider between them. "I slipped in the practice, grabbed a pair of the gloves I keep around for cleaning. I went through the back door and she was there. Waiting. Waiting for me to *help* her when I'd already decided that helping her meant losing you."

While Kenna was disgusted at what he'd laid before her thus far, there was no refuting that the admission was romantic in the most twisted sense.

"One of my hands went around her throat. The other, over her mouth." Dayton's brows pinched together. "She didn't scream into my hand. Didn't struggle excessively. The muffled noise she made sounded more like a plea."

Every bit of her blood crystallized to ice. It would not have surprised her if the final, fading beats of her pulse followed. Scratch the romance. This was disgusting.

Downright disturbing.

And yet there they sat; he, bearing his soul in a way that he could do with no one else while she conjured the stamina necessary to stomach the grotesque retelling.

All around them, the gentle ambiance of nature played out. The calls of distant birds. The whispered swoosh of trees. But the most prominent sound was excluded from this soundtrack.

Two harrowed hearts, beating wildly with the hope that they survived the follies of their minds and bodies, from which they were inseparable.

He examined her with genuine concern. "Are you sure you want me to go on?"

A slight nod of her head was all the consent he needed.

"Everything after that was a blur. At that point, you were probably on your way to the practice. She was small enough so I … folded her up a bit and put her in my trunk. She stayed there from the rest of the afternoon until early the next morning, when I got off my shift at the emergency room."

"What about November? The search warrant?" Kenna asked, narrowing her eyes. The possibility that this was a sickly woven fabrication rather than an actual crime that had been committed was terrifying. "Reynolds was on the warpath. He would've raided the car. He would have found something."

"Had that car been there that day, I wouldn't be sitting beside you right now."

"What do you mean *that* car?"

"I went back to the dealership in Portland and exchanged it. It's a little unusual but not completely unheard of. I kept the plates. It's the same make, model, color, year. The same fucking car. It was the best I could come up with. Leaving anything to chance wasn't an option."

Kenna circled back to the main narrative. "So, what, you have her in the trunk all night," every breath competed against the bile rising in her throat, "and then you put her in the dumpster?"

She was already doing the mental math, contradicting her own conjecture. Lacey died—was *killed*—on a Friday. Her body wasn't stumbled upon until the following Thursday.

Which meant …

"I hid her under the floorboards." Dayton's lips formed a flat line. "I needed time to think."

Time to think. Not time to repent or to turn himself in or, least of all, inform her of what was unfolding.

Nausea consumed her as the realization dawned that Dayton had been worried she was in the crawl space for a very different reason. Perhaps he didn't think she had been seeking out one of his home movies but rather any evidence that a corpse may have left behind.

The air around her thickened and she was choked by a humidity that was too severe to have been real. That imagined discomfort held her perfectly still as he continued.

"I considered getting up early one morning, dumping her somewhere. But I worried it would come across too suspicious if my car was recorded on the traffic cameras at a time that was far outside of my usual routine. After a few days, she started to smell. I slept on the couch. I couldn't stand being in that room, forced to reckon with what I'd done and tormented by the looming question of what to *do* with her."

Kenna registered her every breath, every blink, thankful for each one as she listened to Dayton recount his madness.

"Trivia came to mind as a solution. It fell within the confines of my typical behavior. Leaving her in the dumpster seemed to fit what a scared kid might do."

"Like Sanders?"

He nodded grimly. "As for her being found, I couldn't have known it'd be the same evening. I'm a regular. It would've been far more suspicious had I not been there. I stayed for questioning like everyone else. Kept a level head. Then, once we were officially free to go, I went home and spent the whole night cleaning the crawl space."

"That explains why you cleared out your … memorabilia." Kenna thought it was too casual a word to describe his film collection, but her mind was short-circuiting. Speech was a miracle. Anger knotted itself in her throat. "Why are you telling me this?"

His mouth opened several beats before he spoke. "You asked."

"I asked if you did it, not for every grizzly detail."

Dayton seized both her hands in his and, though she flinched, she allowed the contact. "Put yourself in my place. For *one* second." Restraint reddened his face. Veins bulging. Eyes darkening. "Do you realize the gravity of everything I've admitted to you? Tell me you understand what this means."

As Kenna regarded him in silence, his words from the previous evening floated through her head. Trust. That slithering, halting word.

She studied her monster. His skin had reverted to its usual shade. His eyes had lost their menacing edge. A stray piece of hair fell into Dayton's line of sight and, with twitching fingers, she reached out and brushed it aside. Her gentle smile felt like the final tug on a corset. Painful but necessary.

"There's no part of you I shouldn't trust."

July

2 2

TRAITOR

Kenna

"He's with a patient now, but he'll call you when he's ready." Kenna managed a barely-there smile for the elderly woman, Ms. Gibson.

"That's a gorgeous ring you have, by the way."

Her lips abandoned their half-hearted platitude as she glanced at the diamond studded anchor, that weight tying her to this life of malice. "Thank you."

Ms. Gibson sunk into one of the waiting room chairs and hid behind the pages of a culinary magazine, purse a shapeless heap at her feet. For Kenna, everything felt discordant in the small space.

The flipping pages, too loud.

The air conditioning, too cool.

The ring on her finger, too tight.

She felt herself shrinking away as the room stretched itself out into a long, long corridor; she, at one end and the reception desk at the other. Kenna squeezed her eyes shut and, when she opened them, nothing had changed. Cars zoomed past on the street. The

148

AC rattled. Ms. Gibson still held the magazine disconcertingly close to her face.

Dayton didn't like it when she left patients alone in the waiting room, but Ms. Gibson was his final appointment and she seemed occupied—and unlikely to vandalize the place.

Grabbing her bag, Kenna stalked off to the bathroom, twisting the lock once she was inside. She sat on the toilet, fully clothed, and placed her ring atop the toilet paper dispenser, where it gleamed at her menacingly. It was so quiet that her breath bounced off the tiled floor.

Unzipping her bag, she pulled out her wallet, extracting the card of one Detective Brian Reynolds. Her heartbeat traveled so far up her throat, her tongue pulsated as the phone number stared back at her.

The dial tone competed with the actual ringing in her ears. A familiar voice answered, "Reynolds."

Between her anxiety and the psychosomatic responses threatening to do her in, her own came out as a strangled whisper. "I know what happened."

"Who the hell is—"

She ended the call and chucked the phone in her bag upon hearing the light conversation filtering through the walls. Dayton had finished with Mr. Alvarez. He was likely waiting at the desk and she wasn't there to confirm his next appointment.

Dayton's professional tone carried through the space.

"I'll get that taken care of for you, Mr. Alvarez, as long as Ms. Gibson doesn't mind waiting. Seems my receptionist stepped out for a moment."

He hadn't cued his patients in on their marriage. In accordance with standard practice, they weren't to know anything about his personal life. Even outside of this, he was a private person for reasons that ran counterintuitive to his career.

The digital bell chimed as Mr. Alvarez left and she soon heard the low rumblings of Dayton welcoming Ms. Gibson in, followed by the snick of the door to the psychotherapy room.

Only then did she feel safe enough to emerge from the bathroom. Bag clutched tightly against her chest, she let herself out through the back, gaze glued below her feet, to that sun-bleached asphalt where a young woman took her final gasping breaths. Where she glimpsed the sun one last time as she was stripped of her own light.

Kenna's tears plopped to the ground and it felt wrong, their falling. Selfish. She had no right to cry in that very spot where Lacey's life had been stolen while her family and friends were left clueless and inconsolable.

She crossed the street with no destination in mind, guided by the need to get away. Someone traveling the opposite direction bumped elbows with her in passing, rough enough that each of them stopped. She felt herself blanch from head to toe upon meeting the eye of an East Haven police officer. It mattered little that he was young, puny, and far from intimidating; rather, it was what he represented that had her panicked.

"You alright, ma'am?"

Managing a swift nod, she said, "Fine."

He held a to-go cup from Big Leaf, the contents of which would have ended up all over him were it not for the splash stick. Mumbling a polite word of parting to the officer, Kenna hurried off toward the coffee shop.

She ordered a black drip coffee that she didn't plan on drinking but which gave her an excuse to sit inside the shop.

Her heartbeat shook through her like a radio with its bass cranked all the way up. She sat in the corner, facing the large windows. Steam danced upward from the untouched coffee. The practice was just a hair out of sight, temporarily calming her mind.

Pulling out her phone, Kenna was taunted by notifications of 13 missed calls and two voicemails from Detective Reynolds. She played both.

"Miss O'Callaghan, I'd very much like to speak with you regarding the Greene case. Please give me a call back."

The second was more stern.

"Kenna, don't make me drive down there. You have until the end of the day to call me."

Long after the messages had ended, she held the phone to her ear. Temporary paralysis seized her hand, her arm. She sat like a statue on an imaginary call until she came to and dialed him back.

"I understand you have some information."

Noting the time, Kenna decided it was best to keep things brief. "Listen, I can't talk right now. Meet me in the Roth's parking lot tomorrow at 9 p.m. I'll be in a Caprice."

She terminated the call, powered down the phone, and discarded it inside her bag. It gleamed at her there, in the shadows, and in the span of the phone call it had transformed from a familiar object to a cursed one. Her desire to see Dayton punished had manifested an evil that possessed the device.

Speak of the devil.

Dayton's broad frame breezed through Big Leaf's front door. After a quick scan of the shop's interior, he headed over to join her by the window. As an extra precaution, Kenna zipped her bag before greeting him with a kiss on his scarred cheek.

He assessed her, eyes roaming to every point on her face. "You weren't there to see to Mr. Alvarez."

"No, I wasn't. But," Kenna hesitated, hand cupping the bottom of her coffee, "I needed a moment alone. It couldn't wait."

"Do you suppose this reaction had something to do with what we discussed? Because, if that's the case, it might be best if you start seeing someone, as I suggested before."

There was no masking her incredulity. She wore it proudly, plainly. "This isn't exactly the kind of thing that can be safely discussed in psychotherapy, now is it? Or anywhere else, for that matter."

Dayton shoved a hand through his hair, staring out at the

deserted street as if it held some kind of answer. "Surely, you could get creative with how you present it. Focus on the emotions you're trying to process rather than the event itself."

She felt small on that metal stool, two feet away from the man she loved, yet she felt like she was in another dimension. Her voice was weak, defeated by their conversation and all that had happened the last few weeks.

"I'm not sure anyone can help me work through this. Ever."

Shrugging slightly, Dayton sighed. "Well, at the very least, maybe we can take your mind off things for tonight. Nathan can't make it to trivia. I'd love for you to come."

Dayton

It was odd walking side by side with Kenna into The Rusted Monkey, the site of their tiebreaker. Their drunken kiss in the alley. The former crime scene.

She had never sat with him at the bar but she did so that evening in Nathan's absence. Occasionally, he caught her looking over at The Barenaked Philosophers' table, which housed some of her former teammates. Dayton almost felt guilty for having turned her into a social leper but he hadn't arrived at their current state of affairs alone.

She'd made her choice.

"You've hardly touched your drink."

As if proving a point, Kenna guzzled half of her honey mead. "Happy?"

"Listen, I know you're having a bit of a hard time dealing with everything I told you, but you really can't leave patients by themselves."

She turned her attention toward the long expanse of bar, Sasha running around behind it. "I *know* you don't approve of leaving patients unattended in the waiting room but, come on, Ms. Gibson is an old coot."

He covered his mouth and pressed his lips into a tight line but, even so, his laughter slipped forth.

Defensively, she demanded, "What do you find funny about that?"

"Old coot?"

Though she allowed herself a small smile, she turned serious in the same beat. "Like I said, I just needed to be alone. I have to find a way to deal with all of this. That's all."

Kenna excused herself to the restroom and left him alone with her words. They echoed in his head and drowned out the buzzing bar.

He grimaced as he sipped his club soda. Dayton craved something stronger but he refused to give in to that vice. If not forever, he'd remain sober at least until he fought his way through this mess, this destruction born out of a terrible lapse of judgment whose lingering effects feasted away on his frail marriage like a cancerous growth. That rapidly spreading, vicious rot that promised no survivors.

A ruckus across the way stole his focus at the same time Kenna emerged from the back of the bar. Quiet mumblings from the Barenaked Philosophers escalated to a full-blown commotion. Ivy iced him out with mute fury.

Every Thursday, for months, they'd coexisted civilly for the two hours trivia spanned.

Kenna, he realized, was the anomaly.

As soon as she returned to her seat, it was like some infinitesimal shift threw everything off balance. Ivy cracked.

She yanked away from someone's hold within the booth and sped toward them. Liam scrambled after her but he showed no interest in intervening. He cowered lamely behind Ivy like a useless sidekick.

Below the bar counter, Dayton laid a hand over Kenna's. She tensed beneath his touch.

"It was bad enough that you were hanging out with him,

fucking him, whatever you were doing. But marriage? Tell me, honestly, what the hell went through your head that told you marrying *him* was a good decision? You traitorous bitch."

At this point, every patron in The Rusted Monkey was invested in the drama unfolding between two of the regular trivia teams. Even the music had stopped.

"Ivy," Dayton implored.

Her umber eyes cut to him, two freshly sharpened daggers. "Keep my name out of your mouth." Reverting her attention to Kenna, she pressed on. "You don't have anything to say? Funny, isn't it? The night you swore you were on our side, you wouldn't stop talking. You wanted details. I'm beginning to think you're just as twisted as he is."

Dayton's blood vessels froze over like pipes in the dead of winter. *Our side.*

"Look, Ivy—" but that was as far as Kenna got before she was cut off.

"Don't patronize me. God, how can you sit there with that ring on your finger and that *asshole* next to you and act like all of this is okay? Do you think you're better than me? Better than the rest of us? Let's see how fucking far that conflated way of thinking gets you, sweetheart. 'Cause one day you'll wake up, and you'll be a ghost to him."

Liam gently grabbed her arm. "Alright, babe, you've said enough. Let's go back to our seats before they decide to kick us out."

She jerked away and shot him a cold look. "Don't even try to get involved in this, Sung-Min."

As the music resumed, Dayton suggested to Kenna that they leave.

Ivy shouted after them as they headed for the exit. "I loved you, Merino. I loved you and you drugged me. I *know* you did."

·　·　·

154

Dayton scarcely waited for the front door to click shut before slamming Kenna against it. She winced and then she made as if to back up though she had nowhere to go. Her swallow punctuated the thick silence.

"Let go of me."

Lowering his face an inch from hers, he spoke in a dangerous whisper. "I will do no such thing."

"Ivy put on quite a performance. Too bad my distracted state prevented me from appreciating it fully."

"Distracted?"

"Don't play coy, lamb. It's a disservice to your intellect." Slowly, his thumb stroked her cheek. Once, twice. On the third swipe, he hooked it under her jaw, forcing her to meet his gaze. "Our side? Were those not her exact words?"

"I told her there were others. No specifics. No vows of alliance, either. Maybe you can sleep a little easier knowing a gang of 20-something-year-old women aren't out for your blood."

He released her and crossed the room to stand by the bookcases. Something tore at his heart while Kenna stayed glued to the door.

"On Whidbey, I promised you everything. That can't happen unless you leave the past alone."

From her fearful corner, courage poured out of her. "And what exactly is everything?"

Dayton's thoughts paused. Even his breath seemed to suspend itself in consideration. There was, of course, nothing to consider on his end. He associated their forever with that one word. A lifetime of memories yet to be made, tied up in a neat little bow in those four syllables.

Somewhere amid his contemplation, Kenna had strayed from her post. She stood toe to toe with him. Wild unease painted itself across her face, giving her a feral, broken edge.

"I want no part of it if it means a lifetime of this. The crying, the shouting, the arguing. I won't survive it. Not because I'm not strong enough, but because I won't tolerate it." She stepped closer and their ankles locked. She steadied herself against him in a way that was anything but affectionate. "Hear me. These will be the words that make or break us, not any threat or ultimatum you drop. I'm not some experiment you can fuck and forget. You've acknowledged as much. You've professed your love to me. You married me. I deserve some respect. I am your equal in this house, this relationship, this life. If you can't accept that, we need to end this once Sanders is rotting away in a jail cell."

The brutal honesty of her speech broke something within him. For so long, he had feared her leaving. The possibility that she wouldn't reciprocate his love. He'd treated her like an animal who might run off if let out of its cage, and he'd been too blind to notice his confinement of her had created a divide between them.

She got through to him in that moment, really and truly, in a way no one ever had. Dayton looked at her with fresh eyes, as though seeing her for the first time. He caught a flash of the firm yet uncertain girl who'd flooded his office like a firestorm on a cold January morning, whose presence still filled the room long after she'd gone.

Hands trembling, he cupped her face. "What have I done to you?"

"Never mind that." She lowered his hands. Cutting off access to her skin, her warmth. "It's what you do from now on that matters."

23

SPOUSAL PRIVILEGE

Kenna

Friday evening, she said her goodbyes to Dayton as he headed out for his shift at the emergency room. She remained calm and collected despite the avalanche raging within and whose fallout refused to quiet until long after the door shut and the Taycan's soft purring faded down the road.

Even after it had disappeared, Kenna peered through the curtains, fearing its unscheduled return. She understood there was a strong possibility Dayton had gotten wind of her plans. It was entirely possible he'd ditched his shift and was instead lurking in the very place where she was to meet Reynolds, waiting to ambush her.

There was no getting around him.

He always knew.

The hours before their meeting passed in a flurry of anxiety. Kenna paced the living room floor, stopping every few minutes to look out the window. She checked her phone obsessively, in case a message had come through from either of the men who had her stomach in knots.

Unable to stand the confines of the house or her whirling mind any longer, she ended up leaving half an hour earlier than she'd originally planned.

Pink and orange hues tinged the sky but darkened as she drove the short distance from Fairbrook to the other side of town. In that time, those marvelous colors had intensified, along with Kenna's fear that she was making a grave error.

Parking at the far end of the Roth's lot and seeing no sign of Dayton's sleek car did not ease her worry. She had deleted all traces of her communications with Reynolds and yet it wouldn't have shocked her one iota if her husband showed up.

A black SUV parked three spaces to her left. Her phone rang as its lights went out. No sooner than she'd accepted the call, a voice spewed instructions.

"Your phone stays in your car. Walk around the back of the SUV and get in."

Reynolds hung up before she could interject. However wary she may have been, she complied and within moments she found herself in the passenger seat.

Even at the late hour, people milled in and out of the store with carts and brown sacks and children in tow. Across town, as Dayton evaluated ER admissions, he had no clue—or so she desperately hoped—what she was up to. Life went on outside of the detective's car, but while trapped in its stuffiness and stillness this was hard to fathom.

Kenna shivered as Reynolds at last turned to address her. He looked much the same. A touch more haggard.

"We've been hunting Sanders for months. My lieutenant put me off Merino. Which begs the question, what are you doing calling me?"

She was quiet in the wake of his inquiry. Why had she called him? Between Jasmine and Whidbey, her brain felt as if it were firing on its last neuron. Panic and overwhelm had gotten the best of her that day in the bathroom stall when she'd fumbled for the detective's card.

Indecision welled on her tongue.

"I honestly don't know."

The detective eyed her as if she were a child who'd prank called the police. "You *do* have information. Isn't that right, Ms. O'Callaghan? Surely, you wouldn't have called otherwise. I came here tonight to listen. My time is limited and I don't take kindly to people who waste it."

Mrs. O'Callaghan-Merino, she silently corrected. Kenna didn't bother correcting him aloud. It still sounded strange to her own ears.

Antsy amid her silence, Reynolds pressed on, "I get that you're hesitant to talk, but you should know you did the right thing. You're sitting here with me now. That's the first step."

Her voice became a shell of itself. A hollow, timid sound. "If I tell you what I know, everything changes."

"I was confident from the beginning Sanders had nothing to do with the murder. He was just a scared kid who fled town between the time Lacey Greene escaped from his basement to the time her body was discovered."

The sun had long since set but the sky seemed to grow darker. Overhead in the lot, the streetlamps seemed to dim. Her breath quickened to the point where it felt like her heart couldn't keep up with her demand for oxygen. She thought of her phone lying unattended in the station wagon. Dayton could've been calling her at that very moment. He'd wonder why she didn't pick up. Why—

"Really, it's unprofessional for me to tell you this." Reynolds looked at her and, though his words suggested otherwise, uncertainty was absent from his expression. "Merino and I had a brief interaction during another case. Not a case per se. It was a suicide, but I was the responding officer on the scene. I was with Branch Spring PD back then."

"Bella McAnders," Kenna said without missing a beat.

"Did you know her?"

"No. That was years before I moved here. But it's hard to escape that story on campus."

"The medical examiner deliberated for a while on the manner of death. Said there was something present in the coroner's report that suggested maybe it wasn't a suicide. He went back and forth on it but at the end of the day that was the ruling. Didn't give it much thought after that. But now … hell, I don't know what I'm saying." The detective rubbed his neck. "These open cases just get to you after a while. You start grasping for leads, making weak or altogether erroneous connections." He paused, one side of his mouth pulling into a solemn smile. "That's why I'm glad you came here tonight, so I can finally …"

Reynolds' speech tapered off as she ran a hand through her hair. Faster than she could blink, he seized her left wrist.

Cold sweat slicked her spine as she realized what had rendered him mute. He thumbed the ring and turned his head slowly, menacingly, gaze insistent.

A terrifying desperation punctuated his words. "Tell me it's just an engagement ring."

Kenna looked into his eyes searchingly. Did the detective harbor some secret affection toward her? No, certainly not. This was a man who still wore a wedding ring long after his wife had been murdered.

Spouses can't testify against each other.

Her lack of an answer served as a response. In one fluid motion, Reynolds let go of her wrist and smacked the dashboard with such force she had no doubt his hand was throbbing.

"You *married* him? Did he manipulate you into this? Threaten you? Because if he did, I swear to God I'll pull some strings and get an annulment rolling."

"Detective, I know it's probably beyond all comprehension, but I do love him."

"He doesn't love you. Not in the way that you love him. He loves the control he has over you. He's brainwashed you." Reynolds shook his head. "You're not safe with him."

Her brows furrowed. "He told me I wouldn't be able to testify against him were we to get married. I guess I was just hung up on protecting him."

Aside from Dayton's threatening proposal, she didn't fully understand the legality of the current situation. Kenna wasn't certain she could be of any assistance to Reynolds at all.

His neck bent forward and she thought he was going to bang his head against the steering wheel but the detective snapped into his previous position, serving her an incredulous look. "For someone who comes across so intelligent, I'm mighty surprised you didn't do your homework on this one."

Shameful heat flickered beneath Kenna's skin. Reynolds was right. It was uncharacteristic that she had let this damning detail slip through the cracks.

Dayton had lied. No surprise there.

"Does that mean I *can* help you? With the investigation?"

"Technically speaking, there is no investigation relating to Merino, but yes. Under spousal privilege, you're not under any legal obligation to reveal anything he's communicated to you during your marriage. Unless you do so willingly."

"I decide?"

"That's right."

At the front end of the lot, employees filed out of Roth's. The interior lights dimmed row by row until the grocery store went dark.

"I've kept files on him since we met. Every once in a while I pull them up to add stuff, but mostly I'm looking them over. Checking for things I missed. Clues, insights. Have you reviewed your files? Records from the search warrant?"

"Miss O'Calla—" he shut his eyes and, perhaps not wanting to refer to her as Mrs. Merino, went on, "Kenna, don't think I'm rejecting your help when I say this because, believe me, I could sure as hell use it, but do you think that maybe you're too emotionally involved here to start building a case?"

A cold smile captured her lips.

"Detective, he's hurt me as much as any of his other girls. I've just stuck around longer." Kenna pushed open the passenger door, intending to get out, but she hesitated. "Do you have something to write on?"

Reynolds surrendered an empty envelope and a permanent marker, appearing none too happy at the request. She scribbled the address to the Porsche dealer in Beaverton, folded the paper in half, and handed it back to him.

"Start here. Something should turn up."

Hopping down from the seat, she started to close the door but his arm shot out and stopped it. The detective's narrowed eyes were trained on her.

"Why are you helping me?"

"As much as I love him, he could do with some serious atonement."

Dayton

Though the ER had far less foot traffic than was usual on a Friday, the intakes in need of psychiatric evaluation accounted for a higher percentage.

Dayton was on his toes the whole night. The charge doctors and nurses barked directions in passing, telling him to go here, there, everywhere. It was all swishing curtains and beeping monitors and the sharp, stinging stench of antiseptic.

He didn't mind the night's organized chaos. The orderly hustle of evaluating patients granted him a temporary reprieve from dwelling on recent events. And yet, while he signed off on 72-hour holds or refilled his styrofoam cup with vending machine decaf, that's where his mind went.

Part of him wondered if he and Kenna would ever truly be able to trust each other. Something was always putting them at odds. The past, the present, the people around them.

Carmen was the only person he trusted completely.

That wasn't his choice, really. How do you get closer to someone than the person with whom you shared a womb? Despite having his trust, he hadn't told her about what unfolded in Washington.

There was a momentary lull in the emergency room where his duties were concerned. Activity swarmed around him but he had not been summoned to check on a patient for a solid 10 minutes. Dayton pulled out his phone, navigated to the 'favorites' tab within his contacts, and dialed Carmen. The line purred and purred. He averted his gaze elsewhere as a team furiously wheeled a gurney through the hallway with a particularly serious case.

She didn't pick up. He figured she was stewarding a red-eye to O'ahu. Had she been on the ground, he had no doubt she would have answered.

"This caller is unavailable," came the generic, automated message. Her phone was off. It would have led to her voicemail otherwise.

Still, he held the phone to his ear, frozen amid the ER's frenzy, as if there were some chance he'd hear his sister's voice dance down the line.

Staring at the opposite wall, he swallowed. He spoke even though the call had ended. "I think I may have made a big mistake."

24
GODFATHER

Dayton

Friends, family members, and acquaintances of the Scotts trickled through St. James' doors Saturday morning. Dayton and Kenna were tucked away in the crying room, having been tasked with looking after Isaiah while Charlaine and Nathan greeted the guests arriving for his christening.

There were two large glass panels on either side of the door and, like most new mothers who were apprehensive about leaving their baby in someone else's care, Charlaine's gaze drifted their way every 30 seconds.

A week earlier, upon receiving the invitation in the mail, Dayton had viewed Isaiah's christening as little more than a pseudo-familial obligation. Now it served as a convenient way to spend time with Kenna, who had been avoiding him all week like it was her life's purpose.

His muscles grew tense as he watched her pacing the floor in her ankle-length dress and boots, cradling Isaiah against her shoulder. Here was this woman he loved, cherished, who he'd burn down the world for, and yet she was behaving like she no longer knew him.

The GPS on Kenna's phone suggested she'd gone to Roth's during his shift at the ER. But when Dayton had returned home, there were no new items in the cupboard or fridge. No brown bags to indicate she'd bought anything.

He hadn't tried phoning Carmen again since his shift. Telling Kenna the truth about Lacey may have been unwise but dragging Carmen into everything would have been a mistake of another magnitude.

So as not to disturb his sleeping godson, Dayton lowered his voice. "Kind of you to grace me with your presence this morning. I was beginning to wonder what it would take in order to see you."

"I've been busy." Kenna didn't spare him a glance as she gingerly placed Isaiah in his bassinet.

Busy. Her vagueness cooked his brain, melting it to sticky, useless goo as he fought to mentally supply an explanation for her sudden aversion to him.

Besides the murder, of course.

Dayton ran his tongue along the backside of his bottom teeth. "You aren't taking any summer courses and yet you seem to be wholly occupied when we part ways at the office."

"Do you remember a conversation we had—very recently, might I add—during which I asked to be treated as your equal? Well, giving me the third degree feels like an unnecessary power flex."

"Alright," he relented, raising his hands slightly.

She surveyed him for a long moment, no doubt questioning how easily he'd dropped the subject, before finally settling on the far end of the bench where he sat.

Kenna was hiding something—he was confident of that much —but pressing her about it meant sacrificing all of their recent relationship progress and he had no intention of throwing away that hard-won success.

Somehow, some way, he would find out.

Isaiah's face was a perfect portrait of serenity as he slept soundly within the cocoon of his swaddle. Reasoning that his godson was an organic segue, Dayton gestured to the boy. "How'd you get him to do that? Every time he sees my face, he screams."

A tiny smile played at Kenna's lips. "That's all him. They sleep a lot at this stage."

"You are the expert, with five sisters."

"I'm guessing you haven't been around many kids?"

"Plenty of kids, actually. Zero babies."

"Cousins?"

"Nope. Funny story, I was assigned to a pediatric wing for part of my residency and ended up loving every second of it."

Her focus fell to her boots. "You never told me that."

When did I have a chance? Somewhere between seducing and black-mailing you?

"The course of our relationship was far from typical. We weren't afforded a chance to truly get to know each other."

"We could have had the chance, if we hadn't been so caught up in our … games."

"I am sorry, you know. For the way I pursued you, the way everything went down. You have to understand, you were caught in the middle of—" Dayton cut himself off, choked by the fear that he'd come too close to the truth.

Kenna hadn't appeared to notice the slip or, if she had, she made no mention of it. A soberness pulled at her features. "It's funny hearing you apologize for that."

"Why?"

"Because I chased you too."

Kenna

Her chest felt lighter, spirit freer with the admission. She'd put so much of the blame squarely on Dayton's shoulders, what with all of the despicable things he'd done. That endless web of sins and crime and heartbreak.

Taking ownership of *her* role in everything felt inexplicably right. Like she could breathe, if only for a moment, before the memory of sitting in Reynolds' SUV returned and she was forced to acknowledge the dangerous line she toed.

Dayton beheld her with that jarring, trapped-between-the-slides-of-a-microscope intensity as she watched something akin to recognition streak, lightning quick, across his dark eyes.

Perhaps he'd recognized a part of himself that lived way down deep inside of her. A darkness so granular, it hid within the shadow of her cells.

The door opened and a sharp pain shot up the back of Kenna's neck as her head whipped toward the source of the sound. Charlaine and Nathan wasted no time scooping their son out of the bassinet and into their eager arms.

"Thanks a bunch for looking after this little guy," Nathan said, finger whispering over his son's cheek.

A warm smile illuminated Charlaine's face. "We're starting in a few minutes. There's a spot reserved for you two up front."

No sooner than the Scotts had left, the bench creaked as Dayton rose to his feet. He cocked an eyebrow, challenging her stationary state.

"I'll be there in a minute."

After performing a series of deep breaths, Kenna was fully prepared to join everyone in the nave. Until she grabbed her bag and noticed the glowing light of her phone within. She'd received a message from an unsaved number.

We need to meet. Name the time and place.

Her thumbs shook as she typed a reply.

Come to this address Tuesday: 16211 SE Foster Rd (Portland)

My break should be around 7

Once the message went through, Kenna deleted it. She had followed the same procedure with their phone calls. It was nerve-racking enough that she'd chosen to help Detective Reynolds, but if Dayton were to find out, she was sure her soul would spontaneously combust.

Stashing the phone in her bag, she left the crying room and found her seat among the other guests.

An unexpected wave of nostalgia hit Kenna during the ceremony. The sight of a wet, wailing Isaiah transported her to the orchard in Syracuse. Every O'Callaghan girl had been christened in the same tiny, rinky-dink washtub in their backyard, no matter the season.

Those memories gave way to ones of birth, and she remembered something important that she'd somehow forgotten. Something she held onto until the church had cleared out and only she and Dayton remained on that front pew.

Kenna cleared her throat. The empty space amplified that hideous sound. "Carmen said something to me in the hospital. When Isaiah was born."

Dayton said nothing but his eyes grew softer around the edges. His face lost some of its austerity, lines becoming less harsh. With this softer look, even his scars lost their menacing edge. He was open, receptive, waiting for her to relay something to him he already knew.

"She implied there was a time you wanted a family. Yet you ..." her speech faded as she pieced something together and, as a result, she regarded the man at the opposite end of the couch in a new light. "You didn't actually want Erin to get rid of the baby, did you?"

"No, I didn't." He said it softly, as if admitting it to himself. "The truth is, it was absolutely inadvisable for her to keep it. She was young, ambitious. Saddling her with that level of responsibility would've been cruel, especially since I was unfit for and uninterested in a relationship. We weren't destined to be a family. I called her, told her to get rid of it. I tried to make it clear I wanted nothing more to do with the situation and I know it's not right, or even possible, to equivocate the pain she was experiencing, but when I hung up I felt like I'd lost everything in the span of one phone call."

It was the most tender Kenna had ever seen him. So tender that she very nearly forgot this was the same man who'd murdered a girl with his bare hands.

"I'm sorry I can never give that to you."

"Dayton, I don't want a family."

"What do you want, then?"

The question was a brick wall to her inner thoughts. Her gaze trained on Dayton's face but her mind ran far, far away from that still moment in St. James. What did she want?

The answer was simple. The solution was not.

Kenna wanted to be with him, for whatever illogical reason, until their bodies were nothing but gnarled bone and fingernails, rotting away in the earth. She wanted to be with him, but not *this* version of him.

Her lips parted but no words formed as her thoughts continued their marathon, painting an ideal future in broad, messy brush strokes. She pictured Dayton in a hospital or prison, somewhere he was isolated from society and all of the evil that tempted him. Somewhere his brain would first deteriorate and then rewire itself. Penance. Redemption.

At the end of his sentence, provided he got out, she'd be there waiting to receive him. Her husband. Her lifeblood.

And so she lied, to protect that future.

"To get through Shane Sanders' arrest, his trial." Heart trilling, she wondered if she'd left that too ambiguous. "And then, I want us to move on. From everything."

25

THE TRUTH WILL SET YOU FREE

Kenna

*H*er ankle nearly gave way as she descended the collapsible steps on the side of the stage. It was her first of two scheduled 10-minute breaks. Kenna's gait felt unsteady. Rounding the corner, her stomach churned and she wondered if she'd lost her nerve, because the surety that had gotten her into this mess had vanished.

She finally made it to Portland for a gig.

Throughout the hour-long car trip, she gripped—no, squeezed—the steering wheel with such vigor that her hands ached yet simultaneously felt numb when she'd parked in the grassy lot at the Van Dorens' reception.

Her breath caught in her throat as her feet advanced like twin phantoms and she thought of the wheel, coupled with that sensation, and regretted that she now had nothing to grip.

Reynolds waited for her behind the stage, hands stuffed in his pockets. He wore plain clothes, as usual, and his badge was hidden from the curious eyes of any partygoers.

171

"Detective."

"Please, call me Brian."

Was he making a pass at her? Kenna supposed the detective was mildly attractive in an over-exhausted, dead-eyed, law enforcement sort of way. Even if he was interested, she reasoned, he stood no chance against the competition.

For there was no better view, loath as she was to admit, than waking up to Dayton's scarred beauty.

"That won't be necessary."

Reynolds was visibly taken aback but he schooled his features into his signature no-nonsense poker face. She felt powerful denying the small advance. Her veins sung as if magic flowed through them.

"Thank you for agreeing to meet here. I realize it's more public than you'd like but it provides a plausible cover story on my end."

The detective had said little else on the phone other than needing to discuss new details with her, and that it was best to do so in person. She'd had the right mind to say no. Things were going okay with Dayton. Not the smoothest sailing but they weren't threatening to capsize. Getting to this point had required an unfathomable amount of stamina. Kenna could not afford a fuckup and yet meeting Reynolds had the potential to be exactly that.

There was no alternative.

Saying she was unavailable would've served as the catalyst for disaster. The detective, convinced she'd turned on him, would have then turned the witch hunt on her; shouting from the rooftops about her deranged devotion and sick love for the killer she wedded, doing anything he could to get her sentenced as an accomplice or an accessory or whatever legal jargon fit her crimes.

So, there she stood, playing her part in this twisted game. And, judging by Dayton and Reynolds' obliviousness, she played it exceedingly well.

"Should we get into it? My break is wasting away."

His mouth contorted in a disarming smile. "I didn't have to review the search warrant files. I knew right away your little Nancy Drew gibberish would tell me something about that car, because when we swept the place that day? The sample coming up empty was more of an indictment on him than if we had found something."

"What does that mean?"

"That he made himself look guilty. Never trust a son of a bitch with a too-clean car." He lowered his voice, even though a wireless speaker had taken her place and the Van Dorens' guests were all singing along—loudly, terribly—to "My Girl" and no one could have possibly overheard them. "I have documented proof from the dealer of the vehicle exchange. The car's been sold. There's just one snag."

"Which is?"

Kenna feigned interest while the *clack, clack, clack* of falling dominoes rang out in her head.

Was the manhunt no longer a priority? Had Reynolds somehow convinced his superiors that the focus of their investigation ought to shift from Sanders to Dayton?

"My lieutenant won't give me clearance to track down the new owner. You've been keeping a close eye on the news, I'm sure. It's like a three-ring circus tracking down this Shane kid. A nauseatingly expensive one too."

"So that's it? You're just going to give up."

"There's a world of difference between calling it quits and following orders." A deep crease formed between his brows. "You really want to see him go down for this, don't you?"

"And you don't? I mean, what do you make of all this?"

"It's complicated. Besides, no one cares what I think. My lieutenant made that abundantly clear. If we catch this kid, he's likely going away for life."

"What do you think?"

"You won't be able to sleep at night."

"Who says I've been sleeping?"

"I think your husband was a part of why Bella McAnders jumped off that roof but she wasn't pushed. I think he trailed Tyler with the intention of harming him and that the crash was a happy coincidence." Reynolds spoke so quickly, it was hard to decipher his speech. "I think that after his and Lacey's fight on the traffic camera, she wandered around the corner to the backside of the building to try to reason with your husband somewhere that wouldn't cause a scene. I think he put on a pair of gloves and strangled every last ounce of life out of that girl and shoved her body in his car before you showed up for your shift. I think he drove to his gig at the ER and worked a six-hour shift with a dead body in his trunk. I think once he left the hospital he found somewhere else to store the body until, six days later, he drove downtown and parked his car somewhere free of surveillance and put Lacey in the dumpster behind the bar. I think he went to trivia that night like everything was peaches and fucking cream. *I think* he has a nasty habit of leaving things lying around not because he wants other people to find them but because he doesn't think he should get away with them and I think *you* know that much."

Lenny, the band's bass player, tossed a warning her way. "One minute, kid."

One word, one syllable, made Kenna's skin crawl, and it wasn't even uttered by the person responsible for eliciting the visceral reaction.

"Looks like you gotta get back." It was said so casually, as if the detective hadn't just unloaded his heated conspiracy theory which, in terms of what Kenna knew, was mostly correct.

She was mute, wholly consumed by the sheer magnitude of mess in which she'd entangled herself. A phone call in a panicked moment had brought them here. If only it were that easy to sever the ties. Dayton was to never know. The very idea of it would've eviscerated him. Accepting it as the truth guaranteed the unimaginable. And so it was there, in the grassy backstage of the Van

Dorens' reception, Kenna prayed her connection to the detective ended.

"If you happen to think of anything, better yet, if you happen to *find* anything, I'm always a call away. You know what they say, O'Callaghan. The truth will set you free."

As the detective's form receded, Kenna whispered under her breath, "And secrets bury us alive."

Dayton

In the time that Kenna had been away at her gig, Dayton had systematically torn the house apart and righted everything once again.

All without result. No trace or hint of wrongdoing.

At the church, she'd confessed her desire to move on from this, *together*. Why couldn't he take her at her word? Why did his gut churn when he thought of that fantasyland look in her eyes and that mind-numbing GPS ping?

Dayton pulled his phone from his sweatpants pocket and queued the location app, scrolling through Kenna's recent data. Her departure time from Roth's cured the uncertainty that had eaten away at him for days on end.

Thirteen minutes after closing.

That small though critical fact justified his paranoia. He was certain Kenna hadn't gone into the store and the GPS information seemed to fit that theory.

Collapsing into the armchair, he concerned himself with the next mystery: why had she gone to Roth's but not gone inside?

He stared at the lamplit ceiling. Maybe she'd wanted to get out of the house and the grocery store had been the first place she'd thought of but, shortly upon her arrival, she had realized they were closed? It sounded ridiculous, even in his head.

Kenna wouldn't have left the house out of loneliness. No, she needed a driving factor, something that appealed to her insatiable curiosity.

Even before they were together, she was always sneaking away to meet people. Had she arranged a meeting with one of the few women she'd not yet spoken to?

Dayton had their phone company on the line in seconds.

"Hello. Thank you for calling Verizon. How may I help you this evening?"

"I'd like to request my phone records for the current billing cycle."

"Of course, sir. I can absolutely get those sent over for you. Let me just get some information so I can locate your account."

He was placed on a brief hold while they compiled the records. Kenna walked through the door as the same song looped for the third time in his ear. To his surprise, she dropped a kiss on his forehead before disappearing into the hall. The shower cut on as the representative got back on the line. Dayton supplied his email, ended the call, and refreshed his inbox until the attachment came through.

Odd. Kenna hadn't called anyone that night. She scarcely called anyone at all, for that matter.

There was only one number among her recent contacts that didn't look familiar. An internet search revealed the number was linked to a cell phone but its owner was unlisted.

As Dayton typed the last digit into a notepad on his phone, Kenna came into the living room. She stood in her pajamas, running a hairbrush through her wet hair.

"Are you coming to bed?"

He seethed. The gall she had, wearing that veil of innocence and posing such an inane question. Stuffing his feet into his battered tennis shoes, he steeled his features so as not to burn through Kenna with the molten heat of his ire. "Not right at this moment, no. I'm going for a walk."

At this, the repetitive motion of her brush ceased. A wicked gleam lit up her face, as if she'd caught *him* in a lie. "You don't walk. You run."

There were a million things Dayton could have said, hand frozen on the open door, but he decided each and every one of them would've failed to fully encapsulate the storm brewing inside of him over Kenna's deceit.

"Goodnight, darling."

The last syllable spread like a sickly sweet venom over his tongue as he bounded off into the night. Once he was halfway down their street, he dialed the mystery caller.

"Reynolds."

The voice halted Dayton in his tracks.

He was stunned to silence, standing there in the quiet, suburban dark. It wasn't Dakota, Freya, Giselle, or Harmony but Detective Brian Reynolds, Portland PD. If Kenna had been chumming around with a detective, he'd have a much bigger problem on his hands.

"Hello? Is anybody there?"

"This is Dayton Merino. Certainly there's no need to jog your memory."

"Calling to confess, doctor? Because, let me tell you, that'd make my year. Has that teeny, tiny conscious of yours finally taken over?"

Ignoring the jabs, he pressed on. "I understand you've been in contact with my wife."

"Well, she called me the other week. Said she had some information about the Greene case. But I missed her call and by the time I rang her back, she'd lost the nerve to talk."

"Is that so? Then I take it you haven't seen her recently?"

"Negative, compadre. Unless you changed your mind about confessing, I have a job to get back to."

Dayton hung up and walked home. He idled by the mailbox, waiting until Kenna had gone around and turned off all the lights before going inside.

26

ROSES

Dayton

The sun beat down on them as they labored in the backyard. Limbs needed cutting. Bushes, pruning. Grass, edging. Dayton was normally meticulous about landscaping, but many things had fallen to the wayside that summer.

In a way, the yard served as a glimpse into his mind. It was in as much disrepair. Equal overgrowth.

His hand ran over his forehead and into his hair, sweat sealing it to his scalp. This, he thought, was a preview of the prison yard. The heat and sweat and manual labor that awaited him at whatever facility he was shipped off to.

No, not *him*.

It was Sanders who'd meet that fate.

Dayton dropped the bag of soil. It landed with a muted thunk beside Kenna but she made no reaction. Instead, she continued her task of tenderly depositing flowers in the earth. He admired the sight: knees in the dirt, palms stained brown, the rarely seen ponytail.

This Kenna was charming, sweet. The one who had chided him for using neonicotinoid-ridden soil in his garden and insisted on its replacement, so as not to harm the bees.

Another side of her lurked behind that deceptive innocence; a brave-hearted little lamb who had some degree of contact with Detective Reynolds—for reasons he could not fathom.

Why would she call Reynolds, on the fringe of volunteering information about the case, if not to turn him in? But she hadn't gone through with it. That signified the presence of some sort of conflict, which raised a red flag.

Wiping his face with the collar of his sweat-soaked shirt, Dayton sank onto the back step. All of the moisture left his mouth, his throat, and it had nothing to do with the sweltering heat and everything to do with the woman kneeling in the dirt—who might as well have been burying his aching heart.

"If you plant one more flower, the neighbors will begin to wonder if we're opening a nursery."

Kenna pushed to her feet, a thin layer of dirt clinging to her knees and shins, and joined him on the step. "I didn't realize how much I'd missed this. Being in nature. We were outside constantly growing up." Her focus darted over to the new patch of flowers. "You're right, though. I got carried away."

Following her line of sight, Dayton studied the fresh soil. For someone who cared so much about the welfare of bees, Kenna seemed to care very little about proper flower-planting technique. Or it was an indictment of her current headspace.

He knew her oh so well. She was bold and brash at times but, above everything, she was meticulous. And therefore, he knew, with unwavering certainty, that Kenna would never overcrowd a garden unless her mind was aflame with an extraordinary dilemma.

When Dayton returned his attention to her, her expression was filled with an eerie yearning, as if she'd made up her mind about something and was haunted by the choice.

"I really *did* get carried away. Look at that spacing, or lack thereof. Planting them too close together is a death sentence. The roots get tangled. They need separation, room to grow."

Her words sank in. Was she contemplating leaving their marriage? Was that the great decision that held her mind captive? Dayton assured himself, once again, with the knowledge that he *knew* her. Kenna was forthright. Had she wanted out of their marriage, he had every confidence she would've made it clear. He had bargained to keep her until the issue of arresting Lacey's killer —whether it was him or Sanders—had been settled. But, as he looked into Kenna's eyes and saw how completely shattered she was, he wanted to believe he was strong enough to let her go if it was freedom she truly desired.

"It sounds like you're delirious from the heat, darling. Why don't you take a cold shower while I put on the kettle?"

Kenna

Though she'd been reluctant to take him up on his suggestion, the cold water had worked wonders. Whether it was a byproduct of the heat or pure exhaustion, Kenna's thinly veiled plant metaphor could've blown her cover. She let the gravity of the mistake sink in as she dressed in a tank top and shorts. Another slipup would cost her everything.

Yet she met her reflection in the mirror, the great sadness swirling in her tired green eyes, and she realized that—in spite of everything—her mind had not been fully made up.

That feeling reminded Kenna of their early days, when she'd been equally parts attracted to and wary of Dayton. And here she was, aiding his arrest. While she had convinced herself his imprisonment would be the best course of action to ensure the longevity of their relationship, Kenna failed to think of a worse punishment for herself than to go an indeterminate number of years without him.

Venturing into the main area of the house, her thoughts turned to Reynolds. She wondered if he was making any headway in the case, though it seemed unlikely. The detective had so little to go on. A pang of regret struck Kenna as she stood before the bookcases.

Should she have relayed to Reynolds all that Dayton had confessed on Whidbey?

No, that would have accelerated the investigation when all Kenna wanted was for it to slow down. A long goodbye.

The time passed by at a frightening pace. Before the wedding, it had slowed to a crawl. A day felt like a week, whereas now each new day was reduced to a blink, one which she fought to keep her stinging eyes open for if only to hold onto it a little longer.

However much time they had left together was unknown. Though Kenna understood the duality of her emotions was unavoidable, she hated that their time was spent with one part of her eagerly awaiting Dayton's capture and the other nursing her splintering heart.

Her gaze drifted to one of the lower shelves and a thick, gray book with blue type on the spine caught her eye. In one fluid motion, Kenna dropped into a squat and pulled it out of its neat row. Her fingers hovered a centimeter over the cover, as if touching it might unleash some sort of curse.

Beginner's Guide to Photography.

There in her hands, she held the fabled photography book that Alex had gifted Dayton in that gruesome once upon a time she had spun in their old apartment.

"The tea is almost ready," Dayton called from the kitchen.

Kenna offered no response. Instead, she remained crouched on the hardwood and opened the book, stopping short upon spying the inscription inside.

Dr. M,

Thank you for being such a wonderful friend. You've made this new, scary place seem more familiar and navigable. I hope you get some use out of this for your hobby.

Love,
Miss Guerrero

The kettle squealed as she skimmed the salutation. Kenna shut the book and slid it back into place, then she rose to her feet and went over to sit on the sofa. Dayton strode into the room, carrying a mug in either hand.

"I take it you're feeling better?" he asked, giving her one of the steaming mugs.

She had felt fine all day. Then she remembered what had transpired in the yard and thought about it from his perspective. "Much better."

"Glad to hear it." Dayton delivered the remark without a trace of gladness on his face. He kept his attention straight ahead, blowing on the eucalyptus tea. Impassive.

Kenna sipped the tea, unfazed as it singed her tongue. His seemingly zoned-out state gave her pause. Her pulse galloped, ascending to a concerning rate. What if he had caught on to the true meaning behind her words? She hadn't been very subtle.

As if somehow hearing her thoughts, Dayton looked at her, brandishing a stare that went on and on. Blinking. Breathing. Not saying a word.

Beneath the intensity of that look, her heart liquified and flowed into her ears where it boiled and burned.

She willed him to let it go but it was futile.

Though his voice was calm when he spoke, it was the type of extraordinary calmness that preceded a great loss of control, and the heat in Kenna's ears grew tenfold.

"Are you planning to leave me, lamb?"

He sipped his tea with all the cold nonchalance of a villain who'd just delivered a cutting verbal attack to a hero. Kenna fought off a sigh of relief once it became clear he no longer expected an answer, for he latched onto a new line of questioning. "The cold feet have finally set in over our arrangement, is that it? And here I thought you were starting to enjoy our domesticity."

She dug her heels in, channeling a firmness she prayed was convincing. "You question my loyalty? After all that's happened?"

"One can never be too sure."

Dayton pierced her with one of those looks that overstayed its welcome. His words hit her like a lit match, igniting every single nerve. Kenna wanted to lunge at him and explain herself. Her disloyalty served as a roadmap to better days. Whereas, right now, there was no future set in stone, only the constant torture of uncertainty. She yearned to relay this to him, that things must get worse before they get better, but she couldn't risk Dayton taking it the wrong way; lest she become the second body rotting below the bedroom floor.

One can never be too sure.

"I guess you saw through what I said in the yard. What I meant was, I'm not sure if Oregon is right for us. I don't see us thriving here."

Dayton appeared genuinely baffled, and she might have enjoyed the novelty of it were she not trying to steer him away from her deceit. "What about your graduate program? You're halfway done."

Instead of coming clean about being politely but unquestionably kicked out of Ponderosa—something she'd neglected to mention all summer—she pressed on. "There are plenty of other schools. It might not be the most orthodox thing to transfer in the middle of a program but I'll make it work. I'll start over if I have to."

The promise flowed so easily from her mouth, and yet she had not made one attempt to look for a new school. How could she when she had a criminal husband and a hell-bent detective breathing down her neck?

"Maybe you should take a semester off. We could travel, visit some place you've always wanted to go."

Her heart leapt despite knowing the promise was empty. He was a dead man walking. She played along for his sake, and perhaps a little for her sanity.

"Europe? I'd love to see all of those cathedrals in person."

Dayton swept her hair off her shoulder, kissing behind her ear. "If you put in your deferment, we could leave next month."

Kenna pictured that grand adventure as he kissed along her jaw and captured her lips. Gothic architecture and cobblestone streets. Rivers and mountainsides neighboring historical cities. An amalgam of languages filling the air, meanwhile they'd be in their own little bubble, discovering new places while continuing to discover one another. It sounded like a paradise.

But paradise would have to wait.

27

EXTRADITED

Kenna

alk of Europe had been replaced with calling in prescriptions and the soothing daily grind of running the practice. It was distressful, Kenna thought, that she felt safer there than in her own home.

Thankfully, dealing with patients kept her from dwelling on that grim fact.

"Dr. Merino will see you now, Ms. Schafer," Kenna announced from her station behind the reception desk.

The door clicked shut and she was alone in the waiting room. She pulled out her phone with the intention of checking her email for any new gigs, but confusion claimed her as she unlocked the device. Her call log, rather than her home screen, illuminated the display.

Kenna's heart wormed its way up her throat. It wasn't the first time this had happened.

Over the last week, she'd opened her phone to her contact list, browser history, and the seldom used social media. None of it had been accessed by her. Though, strangely, no one else had access to her phone during those times, either.

She'd had enough paranoia for one lifetime. Besides, things between Dayton and herself had more or less reached a stasis. Kenna chalked it up to a weird technological glitch and resolved to not give the matter any more thought.

Until a banner flashed at the top of the screen.

Breaking News: Suspect apprehended after months-long manhunt in case of murdered Oregon student

She stared at the notification until the screen turned black, and continued staring at the phone long after. Once she'd collected herself, she retrieved the article, which she read with a disarming voracity.

Early Tuesday morning, authorities apprehended the man they believe to be responsible for the death of 21-year-old Oregon student Lacey Greene. After a months-long nationwide manhunt, officials got a tip that sent them beyond U.S. borders.

Glancing at the clock, Kenna grew ill. Dayton's hour with Ms. Schafer had barely begun.

She had to sit on the news for 51 minutes.

Never before had she felt a rush of emotions so powerful. It was as if her body was running through every possible reaction and she experienced each one for a dizzying few seconds before being whisked into the next. But not one of them was relief, nor joy.

No, this was all wrong.

She and Reynolds had sat on their game of chess for too long and someone else had stumbled across their board and checkmated the outcome.

Their plan had gone up in smoke. Kenna felt as though God

was punishing her. Instead of honoring her husband, she was betraying him. Rebelling rather than submitting. Perhaps she was meant to live with the guilt of what could have been. Maybe that was part of *His* plan.

Her mind had gotten away from her and, subsequently, so had the time. Ms. Schafer stood in front of the desk, a garish shade of pink lipstick accentuating her shriveled lips as they split into a tight smile. "Dr. Merino has just been so wonderful helping me process everything since I lost my sister. Heaven knows what I would've done if I hadn't found him."

"He's a brilliant psychiatrist," she conceded.

Kenna fought to stay professional as Ms. Schafer lingered making small talk after she'd been handed her appointment card. And while she felt like scooping out all of her organs over the news, Kenna didn't miss a beat when Dayton came into the lobby.

"It's over."

Dayton

Two words eviscerated him. It was a wonder how such minimal language could send a man spiraling, frantically grasping at air as everything's ripped away.

What hurt him more, were it possible, was Kenna's impassivity. As if this decision had no bearing on her.

Dayton fixed his gaze on her, on this wicked creature whom he loved dearly, regardless of the fatal words she'd spoken. A serpentine rage slithered in and out of his ribs, coiling itself tight. How foolish he had been, succumbing to the fantasy of leaving the state, leaving the country. But, as it happened, what was most foolish of all was believing Kenna would remain at his side.

"This couldn't have waited until we were home? Do you realize what you've done? Every day I walk in here, I'm going to picture you standing in that spot—" he cut himself off involuntarily, throat constricting to the point that speaking became impossible.

"Dayton."

Hearing Kenna say his name in the face of losing her was a searing, hot dagger to his heart.

"Was this your plan all along, you little succubus? You felt threatened this weekend so—"

"What are you going on about? They caught Sanders."

"What?"

"He's being extradited from Canada. It's all over the news."

His thoughts slowed until every molecule, every atom, inside and out, was suspended. The screeching of steel wheels on a train track. Sanders. Caught.

Kenna extended her phone toward him. "See for yourself."

He skimmed the article, not out of disinterest, but because his vision blurred and brain buzzed under the magnitude of the information. But his less than thorough reading did not undermine the gist of the story: Shane Sanders had been apprehended for the murder of Lacey Greene.

He felt lighter when he returned Kenna's phone. His shoulders loosened and his breath came easier. Though a trace of it returned upon realizing that she had offered no reaction. Dayton wasn't entirely sure she hadn't weaseled her way out of telling the truth over the weekend, and that uncertainty goaded him to lay into her.

"Have you found yourself in a state of shock?"

"The news was surprising but, no, I wouldn't say I'm experiencing anything remotely close to shock. If anyone should be shocked, it's you. And grateful to Him." Kenna's teeth sank into her bottom lip, as if to prevent herself from saying anything more, but she finished anyway. "God chose to spare you."

"You've spared me," Dayton said, killing the lights as they stepped out onto the street. He locked the practice and shoved the keys in his pocket as they headed for the car, which he had parked on the main road ever since the murder. "You've had so many chances to punish me. You could've easily brought my misconduct to Dean Raza's attention. You could've sent that email to the state board. They would have stripped me of my license," he snapped his fingers, "like that." They climbed into the car and he continued his spiel while starting the engine. "You could've turned me in. I essentially gave you a full murder confession and you've sat on it like a paid off ref throwing a game. You've had plenty of chances to ruin me. I'm starting to think it's a case of good old-fashioned loyalty."

"Don't flatter yourself, doctor." Her bright eyes narrowed. "I merely tolerate you."

Kenna said nothing on the ride home, though she turned her head when he went straight through the four-way stop rather than their usual left. When Dayton pulled into Ponderosa's student lot, she broke her silence.

"What are we doing here?"

She seemed especially apprehensive as they got out of the car and started along the meandering path that fed into the main grounds. Her expression was on par with someone being made to relive a core trauma.

In truth, Dayton wasn't sure why they'd ended up on the campus they both used to call home. Something had urged him to travel that direction and had sent them sailing through the four-way stop. Perhaps it was because this was his and Kenna's point of origin and now, with Sanders' arrest, the dark cloud that had been hanging over their relationship and their contentious future had finally, mercifully lifted.

An impromptu visit to Ponderosa felt like a celebration. A victory lap.

They paid no mind to the students and faculty milling about, though there wasn't an abundance of people there that evening. The day waned but the heat had not. A slickness coated Dayton's skin and bonded his dress shirt to it.

He stood on the lawn of Markham Hall, peering up at his old office window. The light was on. Someone was in there, occupying his former space, overwriting his history.

"The months we spent together in that office changed everything. I set out to ruin you and, instead, you were *my* ruin. That mentorship was the beginning of an end. You were an enthralling new chapter in my life, but our circumstances, everything surrounding us, grew darker and more complicated. Day by day. I thought by eliminating some of our … obstacles, I was bettering our odds. My mistakes only ushered in more darkness." He palmed Kenna's cheek, encouraging her to meet his eyes. "We've been handed a miraculous gift today, and I have no intentions of spoiling it."

Kenna seemed to weigh his words. "An obstacle? Is that all she was to you?"

"That's how I'd describe anyone or anything in the way of our love, yes."

"How was she in the way? What kind of sense does that make?"

"If you had seen us together, the *state* she was in—damn it, Kenna, I have told you this once and that's enough. You're missing the point. You are my purpose."

"I reject that title if it drives you to commit such heinous acts." She turned away but Dayton caught her by the waist, anchoring her in place. Kenna lowered her voice to a scarcely audible whisper, her words meant for him and him alone. "An innocent man is about to serve some serious time rotting away in a jail cell for something you did. Use your freedom to reform yourself. You need to repent and look within yourself, darling. Only then will I be proud to be called your purpose."

Kenna

He was meant to do his reforming and repenting in prison, but she kept that part to herself. Kenna's hand found his and she guided him back along the concrete path.

"Let's go before we cause a scene. We were two notorious figures around here, after all."

On the way home—free of detours—Kenna mulled over the news and what it meant for Reynolds' unofficial investigation. Would this complication prevent him from proceeding? His lieutenant had long dissuaded him from looking into Dayton and, now that they had Sanders, he certainly wouldn't approve of such meddling.

She considered calling the detective, briefly, but decided it was unwise given the recent bizarre activities on her phone.

Once they'd reached the house, Dayton headed straight for the kitchen. He was still humming with the same manic energy that had possessed him on campus. Kenna stood in the center of the living room, in awe of him as he moved about with great purpose. This picture was a grand departure from the austere man she knew. This, she thought, was a man she could love, a man free from—at least some of—the complications that normally surrounded him.

Looking away from him, she cleared her mind of that thought, reminding herself that Dayton was experiencing a sustained state of shock. He'd revert back to his usual self tomorrow and the charm of this moment would be no more.

Their lone wedding portrait caught her eye, mounted above the bookcases. Tears blurred her vision before she had a chance to stave them off. She studied Dayton in the image with the fondness of a family pet, one whose status among the living had fallen on her. It was Kenna's responsibility whether to put him down by way of imprisonment or let him live out the rest of his years.

But when she peered deep into those black eyes she knew so well, even in that photograph, she spied the ghost of each and every one of his sins; and, in the span of that glimpse, her decision was made.

In the time Kenna had zoned out, their home had taken on the smell of fragrant spices. Sizzles emerged from the kitchen along with Dayton's voice.

"Would you mind picking up a bottle of wine? Dinner should be ready when you get back."

"Sure," she mumbled, knowing he had not heard her but not caring, either.

She grabbed the keys and left at once, grateful to process the day's events in solitude, however long it was afforded.

2 8

ALMOST PERFECT

Dayton

*H*aving sent Kenna out on a meaningless errand, Dayton readied the backyard. He'd prepared green curry, one of her favorite meals, and dragged the dining table outside. Striking a match, he lit tealight candles as the last trace of sunlight extinguished.

The rose bushes were in full bloom, gorgeous even in the freshly fallen night. Gazing upon those fat petals, Dayton had no doubt a romantic evening was ahead.

Shane Sanders' extradition was a cause for celebration.

His pulse jumped in his throat upon hearing the station wagon rumbling in the driveway and grew more erratic, moments later, when Kenna emerged from the back door.

Her brows furrowed as she eyed the setup. Approaching hesitantly, she asked, "What's all this?"

Dayton hated that she sounded more skeptical than surprised but accepted it all the same. Their love was the kind that came with a warning label, one they'd both ignored.

Taking her hand, he guided her to the table. "A celebration is in order."

Kenna's jaw went rigid for a moment before her tongue delivered a lashing. "Celebrate the fact that an innocent man is preparing to stand trial for *your* crime? Yes, that's perfectly on brand for you." Her face fell at once, as if she hadn't meant to say any of that out loud and was ashamed at having done so. "Sorry," she amended. "All of this has been difficult for me to process. It's a situation that should be black and white. All contrast. But, in truth, it's so, so complicated." She leaned back in her chair and eyed him warily. "Why are you looking at me like that?"

"What do you mean?"

"Like I'm one of your patients."

"Maybe it's because this feels like the first time you've been completely honest with me since I told you the truth."

"Your idea of the truth is often a departure from its definition."

"Darling, I was as honest with you that day as I've ever been. You must know that."

"I do," she whispered, tears clouding her eyes. "Still, it's all hard to take."

"Kenna, I know that it's impossible to atone for all I've done but I'd like us to slowly move toward whatever normal looks like for us."

"Considering you aren't going to prison, I suppose we have all the time in the world." A sad smile tugged at her lips. "I fear we'll require every second."

Despite the heaviness surrounding them, she hummed her approval of the curry as if it were an ordinary night.

"Tell me something."

Mouth full, he nodded.

"Do you regret killing Lacey?"

Dayton thought it a foolish question at first until the curiosity burning in her eyes forced him to take it seriously. "A large part of me does, yes."

"And the smaller part?" Her words were all breath. A suspended inhalation.

"I put her out of her misery."

"You honestly believe that?"

"Enough of this." A firm edge hardened his voice, one he had strived to eliminate. "How are we supposed to move forward if you're always looking back?"

"Maybe it isn't such a bad thing to glance over your shoulder once in a while. You might spot something you missed."

Dayton was done with this line of conversation. Their chats always devolved to her obsession with his many wrongdoings. He shifted in his seat but there was no escaping those searching green eyes.

You might spot something you missed.

Cryptic comments were unusual coming from Kenna. She preferred her words bold and bare, unafraid of their consequences.

His worry gave way to affection when he noticed how she was looking at him. This was love, Dayton was certain.

"I'm glad you arranged all of this. There's something I've been wanting to discuss with you."

"For all the malicious things you believe me to be, you can't deny I'm a good listener."

"You are." Her gaze dipped down to her plate before finding him once again. The seriousness etched into her young face was cause for alarm. "Dean Raza, in not so many words, asked me to leave the university."

"He can't do that. There's no legality in it."

"Yes, after a bit of research, I realized that. Whether it was legal wasn't on my mind once I understood that what Raza was offering could serve as a jumping off point."

"And precisely what did he offer you, lamb?"

"A letter of rec for any school in the Pacific Northwest. Think of all the deans and presidents he must know. With my academic record and his personal endorsement, I'll be a shoo-in."

It was easy to read between the lines of her long-winded story. Dayton beat her to the climax.

"You're leaving." When she neither confirmed nor denied the accusation, he continued. "You want to start over in a new town, at a new school. And now for the part you've had trouble bringing up." He feigned contemplation. "You'd like to cash in on the get-out-of-marriage-free card I promised you when I proposed. I suppose you've held up your end of the bargain, seeing as I'm not the one pending trial."

Outwardly, Dayton knew he was holding it together. All steel and scars. But the beating of his heart felt faulty.

"We can't stay here. Everything in this town is tainted with memories of the people you've hurt, you and I included."

"We?"

"*We*. Yes, we. Despite your ridiculous assumptions." Her speech shook under the weight of her conviction. "What I want is for us to be together. Always. We'll chip away at that normal you spoke of."

Every cell in his body soared in harmonious ascension. He hardly believed what she had said. The threat was gone and yet Kenna desired to remain at his side.

Rather than get emotional, he changed the subject. "Have you given any thought to which school you might like to attend?"

"University of Washington."

"Seattle might as well be New York City compared to Branch Spring. Are you sure you'll be able to handle it?"

"I'll get used to it. Besides, I think you'd sooner put another person in the ground than let any harm come to me."

"I won't let anyone hurt you. Including myself."

Kenna studied the table before spying the earth below their feet. A wrinkle formed between her brow. "This is hardly a celebration without a drink. I'll go get that wine." He was halfway out of his chair when she stopped him. "No, that's all right. I'd like to make sure the bottle is sealed."

Kenna

Her reason for ducking into the house was twofold. On one hand, Kenna thought alcohol had sorely been missing from the festivities. On the other, she needed time to corral her reeling emotions. She almost pitied Dayton and his little dinner party. He was convinced he was a free man, no longer under the scrutiny of the law.

She knew the truth, and it weighed heavily on her, like the crushing force of shipping containers, after eating his food while feeding him lies.

Upon selecting a bottle of merlot, Kenna pivoted to return to the backyard. Something caught her attention on the opposite end of the room.

Dayton's laptop lay unguarded on his desk.

The wine was rendered the least of her concerns as she found herself moving closer, closer toward the rarely seen device. She sat at the desk and slowly opened the computer, well aware that she was playing with fire every second she remained inside.

His home screen housed the same innocuous folders as the first and only time she'd used his laptop. Fingers scaling the trackpad, Kenna selected his documents.

A sea of files, and a few folders, flooded the display. Hair rose on the back of her neck at one of the folder's vague yet somehow menacing names.

'Research.'

The double-click filled her ears and seemed to echo there, on and on, as she came face-to-face with a collection of 14 files. 'Rough,' 'Draft 2,' and 'Final' were the largest documents. The smaller files followed a labeling system Kenna was more familiar with.

'Subject A' through 'Subject K.'

She selected the one marked 'Final,' organs contorting in a mix of anticipation and dread as the document battled the outdated laptop.

The first page was mostly blank. A title cut across that vast white space, one that continued cutting through her because, after all this time, what she'd tirelessly sought out was staring back at her.

An answer.

Finding Love Through Lust: Living with Hypersexuality by Dr. Dayton E. Merino, M.D.

Kenna was transfixed on the title, failing to notice she was no longer alone.

29

TAKE ANOTHER LOOK

Kenna

Disappointment lanced through her upon spotting Dayton's looming form. Fear should've ruled Kenna but all she felt was the cold rush of regret. She hadn't read a single word of his manuscript and now it would forever remain a mystery.

Shaking his head, as if at a loss for words, he managed, "This isn't something you want to delve into. Outside, not 10 minutes ago, I promised I wouldn't hurt you, and letting you read this—"

"You did all of this for a book? For research?"

"Isn't that how you ended up here, with me? Research." A wild look came over Dayton's face, and she shivered, thinking he looked rather like someone who had been on a multiday methamphetamine bender who was ready to climb the walls. "We aren't so different, darling. People like us, we're meant for each other. People who would crawl across broken glass with Hell's flames licking their heels if it means getting what they want."

"That isn't me."

"No? Take another look."

It all reeled through her mind. The Google searches. Communicating with strangers. Lying to medical responders. The way she'd shamelessly made others relive their hurt thinking it would bring her closer to an understanding.

Unwilling to accept blame for her part in all the madness, Kenna fired off another verbal bullet. "You hurt those girls, Dayton. Most of them haven't gotten over what you did. Tyler is *dead*. Bella is *dead*. Lacey is *dead*. All because of you!"

Before she knew it, she had shot out of her chair. The two of them circled each other like vultures as their shouting continued.

"I never wanted to hurt anyone."

"I don't see any other reason as to why you would've done this. Why, if not to hurt people? Clearly, you're some kind of sadist, some kind of—"

"I wanted to understand myself. The imbalance in my brain. Why my actions have always gone against my wishes."

"But you're a doctor. A man of medicine, science. Tell me, what's empirical about fucking and throwing away young women? And to what end? So you can have a deeper understanding of yourself? Come on." Her voice grew shrill. "That isn't scientific. It's heinous."

"Why are you reacting this way? You've known about the girls since nearly the beginning."

Hot tears rolled along her cheeks as she jabbed a finger at the laptop. "Not about *this*."

Dayton stood unnaturally still for a full moment, no doubt deliberating his next move. His face softened and his dark eyes snapped to her once the spell had broken. "When we're driving to Seattle, I want you to be absolutely certain you've made the right decision." Grabbing his keys, he headed for the door, shooting her one final, piercing look. "Read it."

Before she had a chance to ask where he was going, he was

gone. The sports car's purring faded as it left the driveway and Kenna was engulfed by the stillness of the house.

Unease studded her spine like a hundred pinpricks as her gaze bounced between the laptop and her phone, lying on a couch cushion. She found herself dialing Detective Reynolds' number before her nausea magnified any more.

Kenna spoke the second the ringing stopped, not giving him a chance to properly answer. "Bri—Detective, I know it's late. I'm sorry."

"Hello to you, too, Kenna. Is this some kind of pathetic welfare check-in or do you have something useful for me and my crumbling career?"

"There's a document. A book. I haven't read it but—"

"Can you send it over? I'll give you my email."

"No. No, I can't do that. He'd know."

She endured a brutal beat of silence during which her heart bordered on collapse before the detective responded. "We're running out of time here. The Sanders trail *cannot* happen. That's why I need to get my lieutenant to take this seriously, you understand? I've cried wolf enough."

"I know you're relying on my help to build your case and I want to give you whatever you need, believe me, I do." Kenna stopped herself from saying anything else, carried away by an internal train of thought as she stared at the laptop.

This, she realized, was her big break. The answer she'd longed for but had not known existed.

The manuscript was *hers*.

Reynolds would have to find his break elsewhere.

"What if I can get a confession from him? Recorded, of course. Then your lieutenant would have to take you seriously, right?"

The detective released a sigh of relief. "I was going to warm you up to the idea the last time we met up but I didn't want to put you in that position. If he retaliates against you ..."

"Everything will be fine." Her body relaxed, a nonverbal gesture of her gratitude. "I'll get it to you as soon as I can."

Hanging up, Kenna plopped into the desk chair. That gleaming white title page stared back at her. Mentally, she pushed away the stress tied to getting Dayton to confess—again—and chided herself for accepting Reynolds' task without hesitation.

The pages before her were restitution for all of her sleepless nights and disturbing conversations. Every look over her shoulder and fearful beat of her heart the last two years.

Siphoning a deep, steadying breath, she scrolled.

Dayton

Dayton was in Purgatory—literally and figuratively—the vampy bar he'd taken Kenna to during their mentorship.

Other than the occasional glass of wine, he had successfully given up alcohol. But tonight he nursed his signature vodka lime, reveling in its almost antiseptic taste mingling with the citrus.

Butterfly middle fingered bartender Kelly had been replaced by another creature of the night. A tan, frail man with sunken eyes who communicated solely through grunts.

Picturing Kenna poring over his manuscript, he twisted his gunmetal wedding band. What was he doing? Dayton Merino did not succumb to nerves. He dismissed the idea. It was the pending acceptance or rejection that had him on edge.

The final gauntlet on the other side of which stood their new life.

As much as he thought he knew Kenna, he also felt there was no way he could adequately predict her reaction to his book. It might have been validating for someone with her level of academic curiosity to read it had that person been anyone else. Another part of him delighted in the fact that she was the first to lay eyes on it. What had begun as a means of figuring himself out had morphed into an ode to her.

A love letter of the most twisted variety.

Dayton prayed she'd parse out the emotions buried beneath all those frightful words.

He raised his empty glass, summoning the bartender, who swiftly made another drink and delivered it with a grunt.

There was only one other patron in the bar, a middle-aged man who sat in one of the two-seater booths, nose stuck in a paperback, which was absurd given the dim lighting. Dayton's gaze roamed to an empty booth, imagining his and Kenna's phantom forms cozied up there.

Everything had changed that night.

The hours they'd spent in this darkened bar, two cautious people attempting to let their guard down—if ever so slightly—had altered his brain chemistry. Somewhere amid those drinks and anecdotes and glances he'd realized she was destined to be much more than a chapter of his research.

She was his supporting data, the very ground on which his theory stood.

Kenna

Of all the things she'd expected to feel upon diving into the book, engaged was never one of them.

Though Kenna hardly approved of the subject, Dayton had been right: she had known about the girls all along.

She just had no idea he'd been using his involvement with them as the basis for some seriously weird psychological analysis.

The bottle of merlot sat on the desk, unopened and forgotten. She'd migrated to the couch. The laptop's fan burned her thighs but she was too engrossed to reposition herself. This book was more than a peek behind the curtain. It dismantled the curtain entirely, providing an unfiltered look inside Dayton's head.

With every sentence, she grew more repulsed by him, and yet every word brought her closer to him. Closer to the heart of this enigma she'd chased down while her welfare had hung in the balance.

In the beginning, the cravings nearly destroyed everything. I had come to a new town, set to start my first bout of employment serving post-secondary students.

This place was meant to be home. Carousing local bars for women most nights would not have served me in a place with a devastatingly low population.

In order to survive, I had to blend in.

He'd had all of this carefully planned out since accepting his position at the university. Kenna shuddered at the thought.

She momentarily forgot the manuscript, eyes fixed on the wall as she pieced together a potential connection. There were no coincidences where Dayton was involved.

Had the incident with the UCLA sorority been some kind of trial run for his later research? Perhaps not but, at the very least, Kenna posited he'd derived inspiration from it.

She continued reading. There were moments when her stomach plummeted and others when her pulse jumped. Despite its academic nature, it was akin to reading a diary.

That notion grabbed her by the collar and thrust her into the past. The memory came to her as clearly as if she were reliving it; she and Dayton, in his office. It hit her in technicolor. Full force.

"I have a diary, of sorts. Does that make me an egocentric little girl?"

He had dropped a hint, so long ago, and she'd been too daft to read into it.

Kenna found it funny, in the most tragically unfunny way, that they had, in essence, been conducting similar work all along, though Dayton's had been on a larger, more professional scale. If one was lenient with the meaning of professional.

From the girls, I collected trinkets. Inconsequential items that would not be missed. Displeasure arose whenever their dopamine hits quickly wore off. To take a part of someone, in hope of preserving it, is to kill it.

It is an empty vessel, one that provides its new owner with no companionship, no relief. And so I, more reluctantly as the years went on, returned to my familiar habit. Through the cycle, I gradually understood that objects could never replace my desire.

Kenna registered that the 'items' he referred to were separate from the Polaroids, another thing that had been taken without permission. A wave of calm settled over her upon realizing there was a high probability her Saint Rose bracelet was, in fact, somewhere in the house.

I found myself in a tough place when my tryst with Jennifer reached its end, not because of my feelings for her but because of the emptiness I felt as a result of reliving the same cycle of high and low time and time again.

I wanted more, though I couldn't define what that 'more' was. For almost two years, I fell into a sort of dormancy. I had a few chances to indulge in my K but, suddenly, I wasn't as thrilled by the novelty of this behavioral alignment system I'd created.

Instead, it opened my eyes to the things I craved most: love and an honest-to-God relationship. I found myself considering, for the first time, things that I firmly believed my deviancy would forever preclude me from; the possibility of having a wife, a family.

She laughed through her tears. Even in print, Dayton was an unreliable narrator; this inhuman monster who could somehow garner sympathy from those he crossed paths with.

Interest gave way to nauseating anticipation as she neared the end of Jennifer's section—he'd given all of the girls different names, but kept their first initials.

The only kindness Dayton had spared any of them.

A third of the manuscript detailed their relationship from their first meeting all the way through their wedding. There was no direct mention of Lacey Greene but Kenna identified a cryptic line that alluded to her lover's crime.

Somewhere along the path of earning her love and trust, I made a grave error.

She finished the book just after four in the morning and

continued reading, tearing through the references and acknowledgements. Dayton cited many people over the course of those two pages; professors and psychologists from his med school days, several international doctors whose research he'd referenced, God —which had her stomach churning given the content. Kenna expected to find a brief nod to his family. She knew his parents despised his work but they were his own flesh and blood; not to mention fellow medical practitioners. What she found was most unexpected.

Thank you, finally, to my darling wife Kenna, for shepherding me home to a version of myself I never thought I'd find.

She stared at that line, reading it over and over. Had she transformed him that much? Or was he simply wrapping up his book with a romantic little bow?

Exhaling a heavy sigh, she shut the laptop and pushed herself off the couch, wandering over toward the back door. Kenna spied the abandoned table, dinner plates and all, and her heart clenched.

There was never a calm moment with them. Nothing was easy or pleasant. It was as if they existed just outside the eye of a storm and were stuck on a disorienting merry-go-round of getting sucked in and spit back out.

The floorboards creaked beneath her feet as she padded down the hall to the bedroom. Crickets chirped beyond the window while Kenna peeled off her clothes and settled into bed.

Her former self would've pulled an all-nighter, picking Dayton's text apart, overanalyzing every line to the point of insanity. She would've called him and demanded that he come home so they could talk. But her mind and body were exhausted.

As she fell asleep, the crickets' serenade was replaced by birdsong as a flock of doves flew across a sunlit meadow, where a lamb shepherded a wolf.

30

WHERE DO WE GO FROM HERE?

Dayton

The heat was punishing as Dayton ran through downtown Branch Spring. An odd feeling came over him while the familiar storefronts whirled by in his peripheral, realizing it was, perhaps, the last time he'd ever run this route. He'd soon familiarize himself with the streets in the heart of Seattle. He prayed that, upon returning home from a run in Washington, he'd find Kenna waiting for him rather than an empty apartment.

At the thought of her, he cut his normal route short. Instead of heading toward Ponderosa, he turned around, running the opposite direction through town and on to the residential area.

Dayton had lingered in Purgatory well beyond last call and had not ventured home until two in the morning. He had slept on the couch to allow Kenna some space. Going for a run had seemed like the perfect way to pass the time since there hadn't been any sign of life from the bedroom. He'd felt compelled to get out and busy himself. Waiting for her to wake up and dole out her judgment was torturous.

Dayton ran his fingers through his sweat-soaked hair as he climbed onto the porch. He unlocked the door and hesitated a beat before opening it, grateful to find Kenna milling about the kitchen once he'd gone inside and kicked off his running shoes.

She killed the fire on the stove as the kettle squealed, taking it off the burner and pouring boiling water into a pair of mugs. Her eyes met his for half a second but she cast her gaze elsewhere while carrying the mugs of tea to the dinner table.

The mood was the antithesis of what it had been when they'd sat across the table from each other 15 hours earlier. Dayton supposed tension had always ruled their interactions. It was the undertones that fluctuated, providing them with brief though much needed moments of elation or passion, rage or defeat.

Entire sections had fallen out of Kenna's messy braid, giving him the impression that she'd slept in it. She pushed the stray pieces out of her face and brought the mug to her lips, toying with the teabag's twine before letting go of it abruptly, as if remembering something.

"Grave error?"

His mind needed no time to catch up to her reference. Every word, every line of his manuscript was branded across his subconscious.

"Forgive me for being vague when my freedom's at stake. If word ever got out that I was responsible for Lacey's death, it would jeopardize the integrity of my research."

Her mouth twisted into a cruel smile. "My love, there's no integrity within these pages. Only the musings of a very sick man. A man who needs help. It's high time you admit that you need it."

"Perhaps you didn't like what you read, perhaps you didn't appreciate it, but I spent nearly a decade piecing that manuscript together. I won't have it torn apart so easily. Certainly not by you, of all people." Her criticism ran like fire through his veins. Still, Dayton was startled at his own response.

"What exactly do you mean?"

"By the person I love."

"Honestly, I found it very engaging but I can't speak objectively and separate myself from the subject when I'm part of it."

"So you see, you changed me."

"No." Kenna shook her head slowly, deliberately, as if she were trying to convince herself of something. "If I walked out of your life tomorrow, you'd still be capable of those beastly behaviors you describe in the first half of your book. Because, despite what you believe, I didn't save you, I merely subdued you."

Dayton could think of no event, other than death, that would result in their separation. Worrying about her theory was pointless. Despite this, he felt compelled to say it aloud, as if reassuring himself. "Nothing will ever take you away from me."

She glanced at the ceiling and when her focus returned to him, her eyes were glassy. "You have to understand what it's like for me. This relationship." For one long moment, Kenna stared out the window. "I barely begin to process one thing, and then immediately I'm hit with another. Do you understand what that's like for me? Being with you means living in a constant state of whiplash. And I guess that means I have some sort of chemical imbalance in my brain, because I love you. But at the same time, Dayton, I wish to God it didn't have to be like this."

He took in the broken woman before him while digesting the weight of her words. She was gaunt. Her once radiant aura, dimmed to a flicker. The fire she'd possessed when she had first come into his life had long burned out. He was a parasite, slowly leeching her life force.

How was it she had anything left, after all this time?

"That book is the equivalent of me baring my soul. I swear to you, there isn't anything else you ought to concern yourself with."

She rose from the table, deposited her mug in the sink, and

crossed the room, where she grabbed her bag as well as the keys to the station wagon.

"Where are you going?"

Looking at the floor, Kenna quietly said, "I need to be alone for a while."

Kenna

Forty-five minutes of adrenaline-fueled driving later, she found herself on the front steps of the Portland Police Department, gazing up at the formidable concrete structure, its flag rippling gently against the blue sky.

Once Kenna made it through security, she scanned the directory and headed off toward the homicide unit. A burly man with a mustache and thick glasses stood at a counter that served as a barrier between the homicide division and whatever riffraff drifted through the hallway.

"State the reason for your visit."

"I'm here to see Detective Reynolds."

"You're better off coming back some other time, little lady. He's slammed with God-knows-what. Been holed up in his office since last night."

"Well, Chuck," Kenna pressed on, reading his name tag, "I believe the detective's isolation and subsequent insomnia were both a direct result of our phone call yesterday. If you'd let him know Kenna O'Callaghan-Merino is here to see him, I'm sure he'll make himself available."

Mumbling under his breath, he picked up a landline. "Detective, I'm sorry to interrupt but you've got a Ms. O'Calla … something or other waiting for you." There was a pause before he said, "Righto." Chuck pointed. "Down that way. First door on your left."

Walking into Brian Reynolds' office was like stepping onto the set of a police procedural. A large corkboard hung on the wall, pierced with photos and ripped legal pad pages containing handwritten notes. Half a dozen manila folders, some open and some closed, were scattered on the carpet. The desk's surface was lost to a sea of documents, some of which were marked with neon flags and highlighted passages. Two packs of cigarettes, several energy drinks, and a styrofoam coffee cup sat in the trash bin, further evidence of the detective's sleepless night.

As soon as she came into the room and shut the door behind her, he stopped working on his computer.

Frowning, he stood. "I used to have another chair in here. Take mine. Please. I've been sitting so long I can't tell my ass from my legs."

Kenna populated the leather chair. She clutched her bag on her lap, unsure how to begin. It felt startlingly similar to the first time she'd visited Dayton's office. The same uncertainty mixed with an eagerness to please.

Reynolds paced in front of his desk. His bloodshot eyes bored into her. "Tell me you've got something."

Wordlessly, she took out her phone, queued the recording from earlier that morning, and hit play. She watched the detective's face closely throughout, measuring his reaction.

"Is it enough?" she asked.

"Despite the startling lack of details, yes, it should hold."

Something ached deep within Kenna at knowing the severity of what was being set in motion, and the knowledge that it was all falling into place by her hand was almost too much. She felt equally powerful and disgusted that she was responsible for surrendering Dayton, the man she'd once feared, the man she loved, to the village square to be burned.

But Kenna had a wild, unshakable faith that his sentencing would allow for his eventual release. And, if not, she'd love him through an acrylic partition until they both withered away. Him, from decay. Her, from madness.

"What happens now?"

"That doesn't really concern you." Reynolds' attempt to brush off her question went south when she pinned him with a defiant stare and a quirked brow. "This afternoon, I'll present the recording to my lieutenant. He's going to jump down my throat over this but, after a day or two, he'll cool off and hear me out." Blowing out a long breath, he tugged his short hair and produced a humorless laugh. "Adjusting Sanders' charges will drag our department's reputation through the mud. Hell, even you know all the resources that ran dry while we were chasing him down. The fact that we wasted all that money, all that time on someone other than a cold-blooded killer … well, it is what it is. But you? You should be proud of yourself. Because of you, this girl's family will get justice."

"It won't bring their daughter back," she mused.

"No. No it never does," Reynolds agreed softly, studying a framed photo that hung on the wall opposite the corkboard, amid his degree and various honors from his career.

It was a wedding picture. Chills erupted on Kenna's forearms at the sight, remembering the story he'd shared with her in the diner. His murdered wife.

That photo forced her to reckon with her and Reynolds' unlikely partnership. He chased killers. She fell for them. Yet, in the instance of one Dayton Merino, they both wanted to see him behind bars, even if it was for wildly opposing reasons.

Kenna rose to leave but the detective's parting words stopped her in her tracks.

"With any luck, the next time we see each other, that scumbag will be in our custody."

"One can only hope."

Outside the police station, Kenna lowered herself onto the steps and stared ahead as Portland's animated downtown played out all around her. Sitting there, she felt like a ghost; her time in this life had expired and she was a visitor. Colors, less vibrant. Sound, garbled. Emotion, absent.

She pulled out her phone and dialed home.

"Yeah, how may I help ya?" Fallon answered before mumbling something off the line, likely directed at one of their sisters.

"It's Kenna."

"Oh, McKenna. Just when I was thinkin' we'd never hear from you again after your odd little visit."

"Listen, and I'm sorry to have to do this, but none of you can come this summer."

"And why's that?"

Her throat went rigid, as if it were filled with wet cement on the verge of drying. "He's a monster."

Dayton

Tension expelled from all of his muscles the second Kenna stormed through the door. That was the most adequate way to describe her entrance; the way she suddenly, with no indication of her arrival, burst into their home and threw her bag onto the floor. She sank along with it, legs twisted into a pretzel.

Dayton's normally underactive pulse felt heavy in his throat as he studied his wife sitting in callous quiet on the floor, wondering where she'd been for the last three hours but not daring to ask.

When her still frame and unblinking eyes showed no sign of change, he decided to say something.

"I've called the shots from day one. It's time for you to take the lead." He prayed that, through his own tremors, putting the ball in her court would elicit a productive response. "Where do we go from here?"

"We put the house on the market. Today. We make whatever arrangements are necessary to get out of here and start over in Seattle." The confidence of her speech belied the apparent state of shock she'd been in only moments before. And, as a result, it was only natural he thought she was joking.

"You're serious?" A brutal laugh rushed past his lips. "Just like that?"

Kenna crawled over on her hands and knees, peering up at him with all the razor-sharp fondness of a house cat.

"Why wait?"

Kissing the crown of her head, he rose and crossed the room, settling in at his desk. "I'll look up the agent I bought the house from. See if they're still in the business."

He combed his email searching for any trace of his old realtor. This, he realized, was the sort of thing any sane person would have remembered. To him, it was immaterial.

Dayton thought their decision to jump-start their new lives might have coaxed Kenna into a similar flurry of action but she remained on the floor by the couch, head wilting like a dying flower on a cushion.

Perhaps all of her thinking, all of the alone time, had exhausted her mind. She seemed to be in dire need of rest and he had no intention of disturbing her.

Why would he? They had forever.

August

31

BOXES

Dayton

The interior of 673 Fairbrook looked like the aftermath of a home invasion. Belongings littered every surface. Books and cookware and inconsequential knickknacks were strewn about. The couch was buried beneath a thick stack of plastic furniture covers.

A real estate sign marked the grass beside the mailbox. The realtor had driven by the day before to slap a 'pending' sticker across it. Beyond that, a moving truck sat in the driveway.

To lessen the stress of their transition to Seattle, Dayton and Kenna agreed to get rid of one car. He had considered selling the Taycan, but he decided to transfer the title to his sister instead— even though, as a flight attendant, she rarely drove.

Carmen helped him pack the kitchen while Kenna worked on the bedroom. Dayton regretted employing his sister's help as he watched her poor handling of his glassware, placing mugs and cups directly into a box.

"Haven't you ever heard of bubble wrap, Carmina?" he teased before tossing her a roll, which she narrowly caught.

She glared at him. "Don't call me that."

"Dad does."

"Well, dad is dad. And you're just a pain in the ass."

Considering the events of the last 48 hours, Dayton was surprised that he was surrounded by cardboard boxes and the shrill sound of masking tape stretching away from its roll. He was certain that Kenna's discovery of the manuscript would serve as the final nail in the coffin of their relationship.

Once again, he'd underestimated his lamb.

Her maddening thirst for the truth coupled with her wild resiliency was a dangerous combination that dissuaded him from making that mistake again.

Dayton followed the train of thought while wrapping his knife block. His motions slowed as he was struck by a realization. Everything was out in the open between him and Kenna. There were no dark secrets lurking in either of their metaphorical closets, waiting for just the right moment to reveal themselves and drag them down into the mire they'd somehow climbed out of, unscathed.

"I'm going to start loading the truck. Why don't you go see if Kenna needs any help?"

"Don't you want me to—" Recognition fell over Carmen's face. "You don't trust me to finish up in here. Because of the bubble wrap."

"Sorry," he said, patting her shoulder in a condescending manner.

Knocking his hand away, she mumbled a string of explicit remarks and stalked off toward the bedroom. His easy laughter carried him out the front door and down the porch steps. With a bit of effort, he pushed open the rear door of the moving truck. He stood on the bumper and admired the cavernous space. For him, it represented a blank slate, the jumping off point for a future that seemed impossible months, weeks, even days earlier.

It has been said good things come in threes. Shane Sanders was in the state penitentiary awaiting trial. His bride remained at his side and, tomorrow, they were heading to Seattle to start their new lives.

Kenna

She sat beside the closet, folding their clothes and placing them in neat piles. Kenna paused mid-fold on a pair of slacks and surveyed the room, the stage upon which so much change had rushed into her life.

It felt odd that she was leaving it behind.

Sunlight caressed the juniper walls. The curtains danced beneath the whispering air vent. The bed was pristinely made and she knew if she brought the comforter to her nose she'd smell lavender, vanilla, and an earthiness that was out of place indoors. She glimpsed at the full-length mirror, at the scatter of nails stuck in the wall where the pictures of Carmen and Dayton had once hung. Now, they sat upon the dresser, wrapped and waiting to be packed.

Her gaze landed on the rug and, in the span of one blink, she caught a ghostly flash of herself sprawled there in a white eyelet tank, peeking under the bed before her head lolled toward the doorway, which was where Kenna presently directed her attention.

"My brother more or less banned me from the kitchen. So, here I am." Carmen threw up her hands. "Put me to work."

"Can you handle the dresser?"

"Absolutely. Unless your clothes are breakable, in which case I'd have to pass based on orders from Dr. stick-up-his-ass."

Kenna let out a soft laugh and returned to her task of clearing out the closet.

"Are you nervous about Seattle?" Carmen asked, transferring clothes from an open drawer to a box. "That's a pretty serious change of pace when you're used to living in a small town like this."

"No. Hopeful is the best way to describe how I'm feeling." She kept it at that, fearing elaboration might have brought to the forefront all the worst parts of the man they both loved.

The universe, however, didn't let them off the hook so easily.

"What should I do with this jewelry?"

Dread twisted Kenna's insides as she rose from the floor and joined Carmen near the dresser. Aside from her wedding rings and the bracelet that had vanished at the beginning of the summer, she didn't own any jewelry.

And yet, a small pile of accessories was nestled in a corner of the open drawer. Were these the *trinkets* Dayton had written about?

She plucked up her bracelet, holding it at a distance as if it were a cursed artifact. Sliding it on her wrist, she admitted, "This is the only thing that belongs to me."

"He's a pig. We both know that. But I feel bad you have to face something like this under these circumstances. You guys are getting ready to hightail it out of here and turn over a new leaf and you can't even pack up your house without—"

Carmen cut herself off. A dour look painted her face as she pulled a dainty gold necklace from the drawer. It dangled between them, catching the light with each slow twist.

A fox charm hung from its chain.

She continued letting it hang on her pointer finger and, for a second, Kenna thought she was going to lunge at her.

Eyes fixed on the fox, Carmen spoke with a blood-curdling conviction that was further intensified by her low volume. "I'll fucking kill him."

Carmen pocketed the necklace as she bolted out of the bedroom. Kenna glanced between her bracelet, gripping it to affirm its existence, and the drawer. Her trembling fingers grazed the jewelry, producing the faintest clinking.

One piece in particular caught her eye. A death's-head hawk-moth ring. The insect tipped her off as to who it had once belonged to.

The other accessories were more plain. Faux pearl earrings. A silver locket. A rhinestone-encrusted hairpin.

They were generic enough to have belonged to any of the Polaroid girls. Her trauma harvesting campaign hadn't included any kind of ridiculous quiz that might've helped her identify which piece went with which face. And what did it matter? They were nothing more than objects. Studying them or finding out who had worn them wouldn't aid her research.

She'd reached her conclusion.

She'd closed that chapter.

A commotion outside jarred her focus. Unfounded hesitance weighed Kenna's steps as she moved toward the window. It afforded a partial view of the moving truck. Dayton jumped off its ledge and stood toe-to-toe with his sister. There was something sinister in their proximity and, though she couldn't see the look in Carmen's eyes, she envisioned it quite clearly. Twin coals igniting in a mad display of passion.

Carmen ripped the necklace from her pocket and shook it in front of her brother's face. Her voice had grown louder but either as a result of the window or through some act of cruel, divine intervention, Kenna couldn't make out what they were saying.

Had she been equipped with her usual calm, rational mind, she would've stood on the porch with the hope of overhearing some sliver of vital information, but the scene unfolding on the lawn robbed her of all her senses.

Dayton remained calm until his sister's shouting morphed into a wounded moaning that rivaled that of the newly bereaved. His booming voice drowned out her animalistic cries and Kenna snagged the only line of dialogue she'd ever salvage from the twins' altercation. It rushed past his lips, rivaling a roar, and she swore the windowpane reverberated in its wake.

She was leaving.

Three words hardly scratched the surface of this enigma and yet she held the knowledge close to her heart. Her chest ached as she wondered—despite having just convinced herself that it didn't matter—which of the Polaroid girls had once worn the fox necklace, for she had a profound suspicion that Carmen had loved them dearly.

They disappeared out of view and Kenna scrambled to the main area of the house, spying them through the living room curtains.

Dayton trailed his sister all the way to her car. She imagined that, while it wasn't in his nature to plead, he was begging her not to go. Carmen slammed the driver's side door and the engine roared to life. He pounded on the window but she didn't budge. The car surged forward and he stumbled backward into the yard as it raced down Fairbrook.

Righting the curtains, Kenna retreated to the bedroom and resumed packing on the off chance he stormed inside. Her heart hadn't removed itself from her throat when, moments later, she heard the front door open.

Dayton materialized in the doorway, face free from any trace of irritation.

"And then there were two," he said calmly.

She offered a faint smile she was certain failed to reach her eyes. Beneath that shoddy veil of amicability, Kenna resolved to refrain from asking about the fight.

After the girls, Lacey's death, the damned book, this *relationship*, she'd had enough of sticking her nose where it didn't belong and dealing with the consequences for one lifetime.

"We need to hustle if we want to get everything loaded before it gets too late. I can help you finish this room."

His compartmentalization after the heated, emotional

exchange with his sister was frightening. It had the same impact on Kenna as watching someone with dissociative identity disorder switch to one of their alters. Yes, that was exactly what it was like, as if he'd become an entirely different person in the span of one terrifying second.

"I've got it covered."

"By the way," he intoned slowly. "You can throw the jewelry out. I don't need it anymore."

3 2

THE EDGE

Dayton

*L*ate afternoon had bled into evening before they were ready to leave the craftsman on Fairbrook behind for good. Dayton spared his decade-long residence little more than a cursory glance before joining Kenna in the moving truck's cab. He looked at her face and his heart, once cold and dark, threatened to swell and burst.

That home held his past. She held his future.

Kenna fiddled with the radio dials until Kate Bush's melancholic wailing poured through the speakers as they drove through the streets of Branch Spring for the last time. They passed The Rusted Monkey and Ponderosa University, real places reduced to footnotes in their lives.

"I'm nervous," she said out of the blue.

"UDub is supposed to be a phenomenal school, and you're a hardcore academic. I'm sure you'll get on just fine."

"Not about school. I'm worried we won't survive this … transition. All we know is chaos. What if we can't handle the calm?"

"I wouldn't worry about that."

"How come?"

"The fact that you're still here is all the reassurance either one of us should need. Don't you think?"

"Fair enough," she conceded.

Dayton's own feelings contradicted his words greatly. As they cruised along Route 18, he worried he'd never be granted the reassurance he needed. Perhaps, in narrowly avoiding incarceration, the universe had dealt him a different punishment: a lifetime of uncertainty. Because, while his body and soul belonged to Kenna, her intentions would forever remain a mystery.

This ate away at him as their journey dragged on and they approached the Washington border. Terrible 80s pop played in the background interrupted by intermittent directions from the maps app. Kenna, he realized, was right to question if they'd survive their new lives.

Dayton was beginning to wonder if they'd even survive the drive, for his mind was doing that wretched thing where it turned in on itself. An icy sheath descended upon his brain, freezing his thoughts. He tried to fight it but it was no use.

Nothing good ever arose from this state.

The one that had taken over when he'd tailed Tyler. When he'd emptied every last breath from Lacey's lungs.

It was this *Thing*, this insatiable need, that pulled off on an unscheduled exit, not Dayton Merino.

Kenna stirred in the passenger seat. A line split her cheek, a seatbelt indentation. "Oh, good. We're pulling over. I could stand to stretch my legs."

The Thing paid her no mind. Her words were static. Noise without meaning.

They came to a slow halt in a gravel lot. A scenic overlook for the Columbia River. He turned off the truck and they disembarked from the cab, wandering through the grass toward the point where the land ended and the sky began.

That was precisely where *It* wanted her.

Kenna

"It's nice to be out walking around. Four hours in the truck sounded like a nightmare." Kenna rubbed her neck, which was stiff after suffering through the impracticality of using her seatbelt as a pillow.

He looked her way but his face was impassive. "Soak it in. We're not stopping again until we see the Space Needle."

"What's that?"

"Never mind."

His curt response didn't sit right with Kenna. Dayton always indulged her inquiries, no matter his mood. She tried to reason through how he might have been feeling as the silence stretched on between them.

Dayton was trying to live and exist in the only way he was capable, just as she had done when she left Syracuse, and she couldn't fault him for that.

For surviving.

But as they stood there, watching the dark blue flowing river, Kenna quietly held the knowledge that his attempt to give himself a second chance was futile.

She breathed in the summer air and for one blessed moment marveled over how everything had gone inexplicably right. He'd go away for a while and then they would come back together, stronger than ever.

Nothing could touch them then.

Dayton's cool voice insisted, "Come, lamb. Let's get a better view."

His hand plowed into her lower back, ushering her along like cattle. Fight or flight activated and Kenna involuntarily dug her heels into the earth but it did little to stall his movement. It wasn't until her toes were inches from the cliff's edge that he stopped. Dayton braced her arms as if this were a twisted trust exercise.

"Give me one good reason I shouldn't push you into this river."

His words made her blood run cold but, even so, Kenna managed to pose a level question.

"What have I done to deserve this?"

"I'm certain you know. Or do you only value honesty when you aren't its primary target?"

Rage bubbled in her gut, skyrocketing up her throat and into the open air. "Haven't I done *enough*? I've kept my head down and stayed by your side. I've been loyal to you. I've loved you, not out of obligation, but with genuine feeling."

"Loyalty," Dayton dragged the word out as he nudged her forward, "is not fielding calls from a detective."

A piece of rock gave way beneath her feet and tumbled down, down, into the murky water. The panic swelling within her insisted begging for mercy was her only chance of survival. A larger part of Kenna acknowledged how far she had come.

She refused to die a weak, spineless death.

"He wouldn't stop calling me. He was still hell-bent on going after you and he was somehow convinced I had information that would help him. I told him I'd do everything I could to take this to his higher-ups if he didn't leave me alone."

"Is that right? There's just one problem with your story." Lips brushing her ear, his whisper, though faint, needled her every pore. "You called him first."

"After what happened on Whidbey, yes, I dialed him. But I ended the call before he picked up."

"You're lying!" he roared. It echoed off every tree, every rock. "I called Reynolds. He told me you called, saying you had information about the case." More calmly, he said, "Kenna, darling, you've poked your little nose where it doesn't belong too many times to count."

Tears streamed down Kenna's cheeks as her heart and bile

battled at the base of her throat. Her entire life flashed through her mind at a million frames per second as she realized these very well may have been her last moments.

"To satisfy my own curiosities, yes. Never with the aim of hurting you, of hurting us. Dayton," she pleaded, genuinely growing fearful as she stared into his depthless black eyes. "Do you really think, after everything, I would do something stupid, something *impulsive*, to jeopardize what we have? I *love* you. Goddamn it, do you hear me Dayton? I *love* you."

Kenna had never once uttered 'goddamn it,' but facing the possibility of death seemed to her the only appropriate time to say it.

A startled veil slipped over Dayton's face, almost as if he'd had no recollection of how they arrived at their current predicament. Like he'd been possessed by something inhuman.

He pinned her in a tight embrace. "Kenna, oh God."

She shoved him away as her tears continued to fall and she addressed him through gritted teeth, venom lacing her tone. "Don't you ever do that again."

Dayton stared at her for several long moments and then they trekked back to the gravel lot, getting into the moving truck like nothing had happened.

Once they were back on the road, Kenna sat in the passenger seat, rendered mute by post-traumatic shock. The inside of her chest felt like the aftermath of a grenade detonation. All that remained within her was shrapnel and smoke.

Pulling in a deep breath, Kenna registered the gravity of what had happened not 10 minutes before. In one transformative moment, the many shades of gray in which their relationship existed had become stark black and white.

Dayton had tried to … kill her.

That undeniable fact loomed around her like a bad spirit, thickening the air, forcing her tired heart and lungs to work overtime.

And then, as if the angels themselves had sunk down to the

atmosphere to come to Kenna's aid, flashes of blue and red flooded the rear window. Five loaded seconds of silence dragged by before either of them commented on their pursuer.

"Of all the days," Dayton muttered, clocking the car in the mirror. His eyes drifted to the speedometer and he gestured toward its needle. "I'm going three under."

Kenna knew why the lights were there. She had been expecting them, all the while not knowing when they'd appear.

The shrug of her shoulder was crucial rather than casual, a minimal effort action that demanded every ounce of her strength in the name of making it out of that truck cab alive; something she might not have been worried about prior to Dayton nearly pushing her into the Columbia River.

"Maybe you have a taillight out."

"We're traveling over 200 miles. I can assure you I checked all of that long before we left."

Dayton eased up on the gas pedal, allowing the patrol car to drift closer, until he pulled onto the shoulder and killed the engine. They were on a stretch of highway that had no lights. The swirling red and blue orbs were the only thing illuminating the pavement, the trees, the darkened sky.

The two lovers sat there in that penetrating quiet, like a needle pricking every one of their pores, and all of the nerves and fear that had been building inside of Kenna converted into a dark festering energy that clawed its way up her throat. It possessed her vocal chords, forcing her to echo what Dayton had said the night of their engagement.

"You're mine now, lamb."

His brow twitched, a scarcely detectable movement, and something akin to suspicion flooded his gaze.

Of all his expressions she'd witnessed, never once had she seen him truly unsettled. Kenna clung to that one, delicious flash of it before the levee that held back her conflicting feelings burst, robbing her of breath and speech.

A knock on the driver's side door stole Dayton's attention. He cracked open the door, since they couldn't see the officer by simply rolling down the window, and a flashlight blinded them both. Rather than asking for identification or registration, the officer simply tilted his head and studied Dayton for a beat.

Raising his right shoulder to his face, he thumbed his radio unit and spoke into it. "This is Officer Hammond. I got a 10-29f out on U.S. 12 with a young woman in the vehicle. Permission to apprehend?"

"Negative. We're 10-76 with plenty of backup. Chain of command says leave him be. Isolate the girl."

"10-4."

"I suppose this isn't in regard to a busted taillight."

The officer pursed his lips. "Afraid not, doctor." Hammond stepped onto the lift and swung the flashlight to Kenna. Even when she closed her eyes, she couldn't escape its brightness. "I've been asked to remove you from the car, miss."

She unbuckled the seatbelt and, as it snaked free of her body, it felt like a straitjacket falling to the floor. Kenna stepped out into the red and blue scene. The sound of the car door shutting was too loud amid the stillness.

"What the fuck is going on? Where are you taking her? That's my wife."

He had a doctorate. She was confident he knew precisely what was going on.

But he was no longer her problem.

"Sir, I need you to stay calm and remain in the vehicle," Hammond said before directing Kenna toward the patrol car.

Soon, a parade of police populated the previously desolate strip of highway. The Portland PD was present along with Winlock PD, the nearest major town.

The amount of manpower that had shown up to assist with the arrest seemed more like a show of force than what was strictly necessary. Eleven men and women to one suspect.

Detective Reynolds was the eleventh, and final, officer to arrive on the scene.

Emerging from his black SUV, he gave Kenna an almost imperceptible nod, expression even. He mouthed something to her that was tough to decipher given their distance, but she was fairly certain she'd decoded his message.

You did the right thing.

How she prayed that was true.

Everyone in the small crowd watched with bated breath as Reynolds swaggered toward Dayton until the pair stood dangerously close.

"You can't arrest me," came his cool voice, slithering through the blackness. She easily pictured an infuriating, cocksure smile tugging at the corners of his mouth. "We're across state lines."

"Oh no? Well, guess what. I have a judge's warrant for your ass, you son of a bitch." Ruby and sapphire glinted off the handcuffs dangling from the detective's fingers. "You underestimated me."

Dayton's eyes locked onto hers amid the artificially lit up night. An invisible, powerful force tugged between them. She wondered if hers held all the things she could not say.

All of the commotion petered out to a dull hum as Kenna held his gaze but the scenery around them turned to smoke. The officers, road, and forest dissipated though she and Dayton remained as one of her memories came to life. She was naked on the dock with Dayton's hand closed around her throat; the more pressure he applied, the darker his eyes grew. Kenna wasn't sure if she'd been on the cusp of orgasm or the brink of death, but she had lain there with him under that starless Washington night all the same. Then, like a glitch in her remembrance, every other second a far more gruesome scene cut in. His hand around her throat was suddenly transposed with his hand bearing down on Lacey's throat. Her eyes went wide as Kenna's shut. Her breathing slowed as Kenna's quickened. The same pair of black eyes hovering over both of them.

Everything after that blurred together.

Of the thousand things she'd expected to feel in that moment, anguish had not been one of them. The scene pulverized her heart. The hurt wasn't lessened by the fact that she had consigned him to this fate.

Buzzing filled her ears and drowned out Reynolds and the other officer's speech. Kenna stepped closer, closer, as if her body was willing her toward Dayton but she didn't register the motion. She felt nothing and instead it was like watching a camera's slowly creeping zoom.

The officer placed Dayton's hands behind his back and cuffed him and though she knew he was more than likely Mirandizing him, all sound remained muffled, as if she were underwater. Kenna also knew people were advised to keep quiet upon arrest, but it was a confident, familiar voice that pulled her to the surface.

"Lord Jesus Christ, you are the lamb of God. You take away the sins of the world. Through the grace of the Holy Spirit restore me to friendship with your Father, cleanse me from every stain of sin in the blood you shed for me, and raise me to new life for the glory of your name."

She found herself reciting the prayer with him, mumbling under her breath. A threadbare whisper that further splintered her fractured heart.

Reynolds and the accompanying officer escorted Dayton to a squad car, shielding his head as they lowered him into the backseat.

The door slammed shut and the patrol lights came to life. There were no tears. No screams of anguish. As the car drove off, there was nothing left within her.

For she had given him everything.

Seven years later

EPILOGUE

Dayton

Prison was, in many ways, what Dayton imagined existing as a patient on a psych ward might have been like. The drab interior and frequent isolation. The occasional breaking into groups for meals and therapy.

After the first couple of years, that grueling adjustment period, he fell into the routine of shrinking other inmates. He was not allowed to carry on with this in any kind of official capacity, but he did so during bursts of downtime and it led to him becoming quite favorable among his fellow prisoners. It gave Dayton a renewed sense of purpose to return to his life's calling and it left him with a deep sense of satisfaction when he was told, repeatedly, that their chats helped far more than any doctor they'd seen 'on the inside.'

Anything outside of these interactions was excruciatingly ordinary.

Out of boredom—or sheer desperation—he found himself more devoted to his prayers than ever. And though he had done everything in his power to get right with God, he knew an equally fearsome judgment awaited him when he walked out of SeaTac's gates in a few days' time.

Dayton had no idea why he clung to the hope that Kenna would be there waiting for him, his faithful little lamb, just as she'd always been.

Until she plunged a dagger into his back.

Seven years ago, when he'd first gone away for Lacey Greene's murder, he'd worked out three distinct possibilities to account for how he had ended up behind bars.

The first scenario involved Carmen contacting Portland P.D. and ratting him out. Perhaps seeing young Shane Sanders preparing to stare down a murder trial was too much for her conscience. *He's just a kid*, he imagined her saying, *he can't take the fall for this.* One cannot forget to factor in their explosive argument the day he and Kenna left for Seattle. Carmen had not visited him until after the trial's conclusion. She had been a devastating wreck as she'd carefully removed a letter from her jacket and pressed it against the glass that separated them, so that he might read it. That letter contained the answer. It cleared up the madness of these hypotheticals.

Scenario two: some kind of mythical evidence had been uncovered that finally convinced Reynolds' lieutenant to come around and label Dayton desirable number one. To hell with the money, resources, and manpower they'd wasted on a nationwide manhunt. Merino was their man.

Back then, in his early days of incarceration, he had considered that to be the most unlikely scenario, purely because he hadn't wanted to give his third theory any room to breathe. It was a betrayal of Shakespearean proportions. What Carmen had delivered in her letter.

The third scenario? Kenna had turned him in.

Later, he found out it was an amalgam of his second and third scenarios. Together, Detective Reynolds and Kenna Aisling

Merino—his darling lamb, no more—had orchestrated the whole thing.

And while he'd had his suspicions that had been what was going on all along, he couldn't bring himself to believe it.

Before the trial was set to begin, there had been a lot of uproar about how the state's case had been built. They dedicated a full day to detailing precisely how and when they'd obtained their evidence and leads. Each time he heard 'O'Callaghan-Merino' slammed together, falling from the prosecutor's lips, it grated his nerves. Dayton had promised Kenna freedom if she saw him through the trial. Instead, she'd taken his away.

He hadn't cracked through the many hours spent sitting at his little table while his lawyer argued and litigated on his behalf. Even with Lacey Greene's parents sobbing behind his back, Dayton had sat there, unfeeling. He had been an impenetrable stone wall from the moment he'd stepped into the courtroom for discovery to the moment, weeks later, he was escorted out of the building following his sentencing.

His lawyer had volleyed valiantly for manslaughter, arguing that grabbing latex gloves in the heat of the moment was a far cry from premeditation. The prosecution had been none too happy with the development. Perhaps swayed by the fact that Dayton was a doctor, they had gone with the more lenient charge. Ultimately, they had decided they'd rather get a conviction for manslaughter than risk a not guilty verdict for first- or second-degree murder.

He said his prayers and crossed himself before climbing into bed, thankful he only had to withstand the rickety cot for a few more nights. His hand sailed over his freshly shorn head and the prickling sensation felt foreign to his fingers every time, without fail.

Dayton's gaze traveled to the window, which wasn't a window at all. It was a clouded pane of glass guarded by a network of corrugated iron bars that served two purposes: 1. To prevent inmates from enjoying whatever view it may have provided, and 2. To ward off suicide attempts or prison breaks.

He never found himself tempted by either escape route. And, though his feeling of betrayal toward Kenna persisted for years, eventually he was grateful for what she'd done. It wasn't simply that Dayton had earned his place in SeaTac because of the crime he'd committed. No.

He believed, with every stitch of his soul, that his residence there was predestined.

The many hours of solitude and sleepless nights had forced him to turn inward, reflecting on his seemingly unending list of transgressions. In all of Dayton's research—flawed as it were—he never could have hypothesized that all it'd take for him to truly see himself would be to shut out the rest of the world.

The vivid clarity he employed while remembering the events suggested he was reliving rather than revisiting them. Conjuring a strong mental image of the women he'd hurt, he tried to put himself in their position. He wanted to understand their hurt, to take it into his hands and mold it into his own, for he hadn't felt anything upon its infliction. Now, he made himself feel everything to ward off the numbness that lusted after his mind, his stint in federal prison taking its toll. Dayton wouldn't allow himself to be so easily overtaken by madness, not when he'd spent his career— his whole life—at war with it.

Clasping his hands over his chest, his thoughts drifted to Kenna. He wondered where she was and how she spent her days. Who had she become? Were they to see each other again, would he find traces of the woman he loved, or would she be unrecogniz- able? The idea that, in his seven-year absence, he could have lost the one most dear to him turned his stomach. There was certainly evidence that pointed to the possibility.

Kenna used to visit every two weeks. Even during the year he refused to speak to her, she showed up and regaled him with stories from school and her side gig as a virtual counselor. Sometimes, she'd bring a paper she was particularly proud of and read it aloud, her face falling upon its conclusion when Dayton offered none of the feedback she still craved from him. When he started talking to her again, she visited less often. Once a month.

Six months ago, she stopped coming altogether.

He wondered if it was a means of punishment or if she'd moved on from him, from everything they had been; and he desperately wished it was the former. Had he suspected there was any chance his life post-release wouldn't include Kenna, he would have taken his own life by now.

Instead, Dayton waited patiently, day after day, praying that each nightfall brought him that much closer to seeing her beautiful face. That darling girl whose love was so beatific, so pure, that he'd committed his crimes in the name of holding onto it just a little bit longer.

Kenna

She often had dreams about the trial.

How it had felt to sit among the Polaroid girls, that gallery of living ghosts. They sat together in the courtroom for a month, often squeezing each other's hands. Occasionally, they offered kind words or extended a tissue whenever one of them lost their composure. A tissue was never passed Kenna's way. She had orchestrated all of this, and she looked on with an impartial eye; though, the same could not be said for her heart.

For a long time, Kenna thought she'd loved Dayton, but she didn't understand the real meaning of love until she was faced with his absence.

Her heart no longer beat. Rather, it burned in her chest. A fiery inferno that left the organ charred and crumbling at the end of each day, only to rise like a phoenix and begin anew when she rose the following morning. It was an ongoing, painful cycle of life and death. Love and loss.

That was why Kenna had stopped visiting him six months ago. Staring at his diminished, changed face—the face of the man she loved—through that thick, glass partition was too much to bear. Each visitation was as cruel as an open-casket funeral, the pain of knowing your loved one was right there while also knowing it was impossible to reach them.

When Dayton had gone away to SeaTac, she'd gone through with the move to Seattle and had begun at the University of Washington the spring following his arrest. After staying in a hotel for several weeks and persistently posting on campus bulletin boards that she was in need of a roommate, Kenna moved into a small house in Ravenna with two other grad students.

While she had once joked with Dayton that six years of school was enough, she feared what her life after university might be like, and so she pursued a Ph.D. in clinical psychology. Mostly, she entered the program for herself, but part of her hoped Dayton would be proud of the path she'd chosen, especially since he'd long appreciated her academic inclination.

In addition to her studies, she'd taken to finishing his manuscript. Scholarly publishers were actually interested in acquiring it now that its author was a convicted killer who'd received no shortage of media attention, at least on the West Coast. Kenna had been asked to write the foreward since she was the primary subject of its text.

When I was approached and asked to write this foreward, I almost said no. The purpose of a foreward is to essentially endorse or praise the author, and I am perhaps not the best person for this task. If you happen to know anything about me or my relationship to the author, then you know why.

So, why did I accept?

While I've admitted that I'm not the best candidate, I also acknowledge—with the acceptance of its irony—that there is, in fact, no one better.

My first meeting with Dr. Merino left me disturbed. And completely awestruck. I battled those feelings over the course of two years, and made room for many more. Love included. But despite all of my fighting and searching, when I initially read this manuscript, my worst fear was confirmed: while I knew and loved Dr. Merino, I didn't understand him.

I was much too close to him to see him for who he was.

No matter what anyone thinks, that will always be my sorest regret— not the fact that I played a role in his capture.

For Kenna's compliance with the request, and for the invaluable role she played in helping prepare the book for publication, she was awarded partial writing credit.

On the front cover, as well as the interior title page, her name appeared below Dr. Dayton E. Merino, M.D., in a much smaller font. Including his credentials had initially caused some uproar within the publishing house as well as the psychological community, since his conviction had stripped him of his psychiatric license, thereby revoking his right to practice. Eventually, the publisher decided to keep the title, reasoning that he still held the degree.

Within the first month of *Finding Love Through Lust*'s release, Kenna wandered into different bookstores, searching for it among the shelves and repeating the same process each time. She traced his name before letting her fingers hover above her own. Then, she turned it over and skimmed the author's biography.

Dr. Dayton E. Merino grew up in Eugene, Oregon. He earned his M.D. from the David Geffen School of Medicine at UCLA and returned to his home state to practice psychiatry. In 2022, he was convicted for the murder of Lacey Greene, who had briefly been under his care. He is currently serving out a seven-year sentence at Federal Detention Center SeaTac.

Finally, she studied the picture beside the biography. It was a professional quality, close-up headshot from their wedding day. His dark hair fell just past his ears and he stared into the camera with his pitch-black eyes, mouth in a flat line that betrayed no emotion. Scars streaking across his skin like a smudge across a masterful painting.

The photograph was bizarre, considering the occasion on which it had been taken. Not that their wedding had possessed the usual celebratory quality carried by such events.

While Dayton seemed to not display any emotion in the photo, Kenna knew him well enough to see through the mask. He looked like a man awaiting a grim fate.

As she waited beyond the detention center's electronic gates, she wondered how much he had changed since she'd seen him last, if he'd continued to wither and fade. Kenna had arrived 45 minutes early, if for no other reason than to stand before the entrance and allow her heart a chance to compose itself for the reunion.

Several people passed her on the sidewalk, telling her that she needed an appointment or some form of clearance if she wished to go inside.

"I'm not going in," she told them simply.

She had not spent the last seven years imagining this moment, but it had usurped her every waking thought that week. The topic had been forbidden from her mind up to that point, fearing what might have become of her mental faculties had she been free to daydream about it whenever she pleased.

Standing there, Kenna felt invigorated with a new strength. She'd shed the shell of the daring 20-something girl in her descent to the darkest places and had returned to the light as something greater, equipped with a fuller understanding.

She now understood what it was like to be ripped apart entirely and somehow come together whole again.

When she spotted Dayton across the way, her pulse seized in her throat. A guard escorted him out of the building and through the parking lot. His grip remained cuffed on his bicep even while he keyed in the code to open the gates. They parted with a loud buzz and the guard finally released his hold on Dayton.

The beating of her heart rivaled that of a war drum as Kenna took in the changed image of the man who had altered the course of her life.

His face was familiar yet different. It now had a gaunt quality that gave him a look of permanent solemnity. The scars, of course, remained.

She found herself reaching for those marks, as if touching them had the power to transport them back to their old, shared reality, eschewing this new, uncertain one.

Dayton almost jerked away from the touch. He beheld her with skepticism, whispering, "You came."

"You weren't expecting me?" Tentatively, she extended her left hand toward him. The midday sun glinted off the wedding band and engagement ring she wore. "I've never taken them off. All this time."

Tears flooded his black eyes. "Then why—"

Glancing at the building, Kenna said, "Don't you see? This is what you needed, darling. You could've continued living a life of sin, but God has given you a second chance. *I've* given you a second chance."

He released her hand and fell to his knees on the concrete, peering up at her as if she were a deity.

"I lied to you, manipulated you, hurt you, *used* you. Yet you're still here, waiting for me. I am truly sorry, lamb. For everything. I realize sorry isn't enough, so I'll keep apologizing to you, I'll keep loving you, until I take my final breath."

Kenna didn't know if she believed him, even then, but she knew—as surely as she would die—that she loved him with a ferocity that discounted all else.

"Let's go home, Dr. Merino."

If you enjoyed the final installment of Confessional, please consider leaving it a review on Amazon, Goodreads, or your vendor of choice. Reviews help indie authors gain visibility and expand their readership.

Sign up for my newsletter to stay up to date on new releases, cover reveals, beta opportunities, and more!

ACKNOWLEDGMENTS

Nearly five years ago, I had an idea for a romantic comedy set at a university involving a bored guidance counselor sleeping his way through the alphabet. Now, it was winter and you can blame seasonal affective disorder if you must, but I said to myself, 'wait, what if this gets dark instead?'

That single 'what if' was the lightbulb moment that propelled me into writing *Darling Descent*. Originally, when I was penning Dr. Merino and Kenna's first book, I had no idea that there would be a second (certainly not a third).

Darling Descent and *Sinner's Saint* poured out of me, but I had a much different experience writing *Harrowed Hearts*. Unpleasant developments in my personal life, paired with the mounting pressure of creating the conclusion of a series, left me with a vicious case of writer's block.

While writing its predecessors was as easy as breathing, not one second of drafting *Harrowed Hearts* was without its problems; because of that, it is also my proudest accomplishment as an author. I am pleased to have made it through to these acknowledgements and to finally have shared it with all of you.

What's next from me? Well, let's just say we're leaving dark romance behind. For now.

Special thanks to my husband, Justin, who graciously provides the copy-editing for all of my books.

Thank you to the wonderful cover design team over at Books and Moods for lending their incredible talent to this series.

I'd like to extend my thanks to Shamika Lindsay and Wesley Parker, both of whom provided invaluable feedback during the beta phases for the first two books.

Thank you to my virtual writing buddies, including but not limited to Dave Ayala, Rietta Boksha, Amber Hook, Megan Montgomery, Meg Murray, and Lanona Walker.

And, finally, to the readers. Thank you for choosing to take this journey with me (and for still reading this book even though it was released a couple of years after it was supposed to … you rock). What I do would not be possible with you.

ABOUT THE AUTHOR

Leighann Hart is the author of the Rosenfeld duet and the Confessional trilogy. She is a huge mental health advocate and this sometimes—okay, oftentimes—bleeds into her love stories.

She consumes heinous amounts of espresso and pays tithe daily to the New York Times Spelling Bee. Her biggest regret is that she probably will not meet Rick Moranis before he dies.

Leighann lives with her husband, daughter, and Sugar the Shetland Sheepdog in a convection oven—er, Georgia.

Connect with Leighann Online

www.leighannhart.com
leighanniswriting@gmail.com
Goodreads @ Leighann Hart
BookBub @ leighannhart

www.ingramcontent.com/pod-product-compliance
Lightning Source LLC
Chambersburg PA
CBHW061546210726
48287CB00006B/2089